The Exposed

Even the book morphs!
Flip the pages
and check it out!

Look for other **ANIMORPHS**® titles by K.A. Applegate:

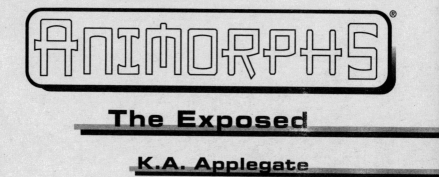

ANIMORPHS®

The Exposed

K.A. Applegate

AN
APPLE
PAPERBACK

SCHOLASTIC INC.
New York Toronto London Auckland Sydney
Mexico City New Delhi Hong Kong

Cover illustration by David B. Mattingly

ISBN 0-590-76260-5

12 11 10 9 8 7 6 5 4 3 2 1   9/9 0 1 2 3 4/0

Printed in the U.S.A.   40

First Scholastic printing, March 1999

For Michael and Jake

The Exposed

CHAPTER 1

My name is Rachel.

I'm tall. I'm blond. And I'm standing on a balance beam, trying to get up the nerve to do a forward roll.

Trying to be normal.

Although when you think about it, what's normal about a human somersaulting along on a slippery, narrow, wooden tightrope?

Nothing, that's what. Forget the forward roll.

Hey, reckless in battle keeps me alive. Reckless in the gym just breaks bones.

And to keep fighting, I need to stay in one piece. Survival always comes first. So you know I won't tell you my last name or where I live. That information would get me and my friends killed.

1

Not that we'd go down without a fight, of course, but still . . .

We're five kids and an Andalite who, as I see it, have to hold on to the three major things we've got going for us.

The ability to morph by acquiring animal DNA.

Anonymity. Nobody knows who we are.

The home team advantage.

So far, it's been enough to keep us alive and to seriously aggravate the Yeerks, a parasitic species here to enslave Earth.

If the Yeerks had a "Most Wanted" list, we would top it. They want us bad. Maybe they'd kill us. Maybe they'd do what they've done to so many humans: crawl into our heads and take over our brains. Make us Controllers.

A Controller is someone enslaved by a Yeerk, and they're everywhere. They're people you know. People you trust.

Our vice principal, Mr. Chapman.

My cousin, Tom.

Teachers, TV anchorwomen, cops, FedEx drivers, waiters, students, construction workers. All walking around like they're perfectly normal. Persuading their friends and families to join The Sharing, the Yeerks' cover organization.

And once you're in, there's usually only one way out.

You become a Controller.

2

You walk and talk the same. You have the same memories. You still chew gum in class and toss brussels sprouts back into the serving bowl when you think your mother isn't looking.

Only it isn't you doing any of it. The real you is caged up inside your head, helpless, screaming silently at the Yeerk slug holding you hostage.

Become a Controller, and you have no will of your own.

I will never surrender my free will.

This is why we fight. And to be honest, I like a good fight. The adrenaline spike of battle. The rush. The challenge.

And now that I've admitted that, I'll admit something else: Lately, it's been scaring me that I like it. That I look forward to it so much.

My father thinks I'm as tough as any boy. My cousin Jake says my specialty is kicking butt. Marco calls me Xena, Warrior Princess, and jokes that I'm always the first to want to fight.

He's right. I'm front and center. Head of the line. "Let's do it," I've said, more times than I can count.

And I'm afraid that if I keep giving in to the urge, sooner or later I'll forget how to do anything else. Forget how to do the things I used to like to do.

I used to love gymnastics. Not the balance beam, exactly. I'm talking about the powerful feeling I got working the parallel bars. And vaulting was as close as I'd ever come to flying.

Not anymore, of course. Not since I became an Animorph. The thrill of vaulting doesn't even come close to the thrill of soaring as a bald eagle. Or zipping around as a fly. And human muscles are pathetic after experiencing a cat's liquid grace. Or becoming a grizzly bear. Now we're talking power.

I can't help myself. It's like I'm addicted or something. Addicted to danger. Addicted to defeating the Yeerk invaders.

And addicted in my dreams, at least, to smearing Visser Three across the pavement like the overgrown slug that he is.

See? I told you I was starting to scare me.

Visser Three is evil. Merciless. Ruthless. Cruel. He's the only Yeerk with the power to morph, the only Andalite-Controller. He's in charge of the invasion of Earth and he takes his job very seriously.

So do I.

"Hey, Rachel!"

My head jerked up, shattering my concentration. The gymnastics studio zapped back into focus.

Kids talking. Laughing. Doing back bends and walkovers. Working out on the parallel bars and rings.

A guy named T. T. was smiling and coming toward me across the mats. Not an ugly guy. Not at all.

I didn't smile back. Until he'd yelled, I'd been doing fine. But now my body was swaying and my balance was broken. My arms began to windmill and my bare feet, one placed before the other on the narrow beam, were wobbling.

I was going to fall.

"Don't worry," he said, jogging up. "I'll catch you."

Oh, great. Just what I didn't need. I swiveled, trying to push off and jump.

Bad move.

The motion sent me reeling. I pitched sideways.

I knocked T. T.'s outstretched arms aside and hit the mat.

Whumpf!

Ouch.

My palms stung. So did my hip.

"You okay?" he asked, putting out his hand.

"Yeah." I ignored it. Got up.

My face was hot. I don't like to look stupid. And now I did, and it was all his fault.

I looked at him, annoyed. Ready to tell him off.

And stopped.

He was definitely not uncute.

He was taller than me. Blue eyes, like me. Dimples, not like me.

"So, I guess this means you're falling for me, huh?" he asked, grinning. "Want to go to a movie or something?"

CHAPTER 2

"Say what?" I snapped.

He leaned against the balance beam, cocky and relaxed. "I wondered if you wanted to go to the movies or something."

I looked at him. That wasn't all he'd said. And the rest of it, the part about me falling for him, made me uneasy.

He was cute.

Better still, he was human.

See, if T. T. and I went to a ninety-minute movie, we could go for pizza afterward. Or to McDonald's. Or whatever.

He wouldn't have to demorph back into a red-tailed hawk before the two-hour deadline.

Going out with T. T. would be normal. Maybe even fun. No tension. No fear.

"Well?" he said.

"In your dreams," I said abruptly, wheeling and heading across the mats to the locker room. He didn't try to stop me.

I shoved open the door.

BOOM!

It bounced off the cement wall.

The locker room was empty. Echoey.

Good. I wasn't in the mood to deal with people right now. I didn't like the way I was feeling. I didn't like that I had reacted. I didn't like the moment of hesitation, the moment when I considered the fact that I was the only girl in school whose . . . I guess "boyfriend" was . . . how should I put it . . . a *bird*.

I felt anger bubbling up inside me. Mad at T. T., mad at Tobias. Mad at myself. Why had I hesitated?

"Gee, I don't know, Rachel," I muttered under my breath. "Maybe because T. T. doesn't have a beak. Maybe that's it."

I yanked on jeans and zipped my jacket up over my bodysuit. Jammed my feet into socks and running shoes.

Why hadn't I said *yes*?

That was easy. Because I'm all kinds of things, some of them not too great, but I'm not disloyal. I don't betray people. Especially not Tobias.

And yet the images in my mind would not go away. Especially images of eyes that would look into mine and not glare with the furious intensity of a predator.

I was going . . . if you can even use that word . . . with a guy who spent most of his time riding the thermals, talking in thought-speak, and eating small mammals.

A guy with feathers. Talons. A fierce, curved beak.

And sometimes, for almost two hours at a shot, unruly dirty-blond hair and hurt, tender, hopeful eyes.

He's my friend. My fellow warrior.

We fly together. Fight Yeerks together.

We are not normal kids.

I laughed suddenly and some girl stared at me. Yeah, not normal would be the understatement of all time.

I headed outside and looked up at the sky, the way I always do. Looking for the familiar silhouette against a blue sky. Looking for the faint tinge of red in tail feathers.

But Tobias wasn't there, and I was disappointed. Oh well, he was probably off eating a baby rabbit or something. Normal red-tailed hawk behavior.

Maybe there was more than one kind of normal.

And maybe I'd just better find a way to live with it. Find a way to really enjoy something besides fighting.

Gymnastics hadn't done it for me. Not today.

But shopping might.

I headed for the mall.

There are few emotional problems that can't be made better by shopping Old Navy and Express.

I jogged most of the way and felt the familiar flood of relief mixed with anticipation as I slipped into the air-conditioning.

Ahhh.

Colored lights. Music. People talking. Laughing. All united in a common goal.

Shopping.

I targeted The Limited. Went straight into the store and checked their sale racks. Nothing good, but no problem. Next.

I swung out of The Limited and nearly rammed into Cassie. "Cassie! What're you doing here?" I said. "Why didn't you tell me you were going shopping?"

"Which question do you want me to answer first?" Cassie asked, laughing and tucking her bag under her arm.

"Either. Both," I said, pouncing on the bag and tugging it free. "Ooh, The Body Shop. Cool. What'd you get?"

"Bath oil for my mother's birthday," she said. "Uh, Rachel?"

"What?" I said. Her eyes were wide. I followed the direction of her gaze.

Erek the Chee was standing in front of The Gap.

"So Erek's shopping," I said, shrugging. "So what? Question is, what's he think he's gonna find at Nine West? A nice pair of sandals?"

"Look," she whispered. "It's happening again!"

Erek flickered. His human-hologram blurred. Faded.

Revealing, for an instant, the real Erek the Chee.

The android.

CHAPTER 3

"Whoa! That can't be good," I said.

"What're we gonna do?" Cassie said, as Erek's hologram shimmered again. "We can't let —"

"Ears all around us," I warned. She fell silent.

Erek is an android. Part of an android species created to be a nonviolent companion to the Pemalites, a peaceful race that was wiped out by the Howlers.

Erek is an anti-Yeerk spy. Also a friend.

"Rachel, we have to *do* something," Cassie whispered.

"Yeah. Let's move."

Erek's hologram — the illusion of a normal boy — dimmed, exposing his interlocking steel and ivory plates.

"We have to look cool. Natural," Cassie cautioned.

Right.

We wove through the crowd and moved close to block Erek from view.

"Hi, Erek," I said. "What's up? Aside from the fact that you look like TV during a lightning storm."

He looked at me.

And he looked scared.

"Erek, you have to get out of here. Something's wrong with your hologram."

"I know," he muttered, hunching his shoulders like he was trying to disappear down into them. "I kind of noticed. Can't seem to fix it. I have tried running every —"

"Yeah, tell me all about it later. Come on, we have to get you out of here," I interrupted, seizing his arm. His human hologram had just gone sheer, like a movie projected onto a screen. The force field was gone altogether. My fingers closed on steel, not projected human flesh.

"Where are we going?" Cassie demanded.

"How can you hide me?" He was dragging, barely able to keep his legs moving. Like some big, overgrown baby working on his first steps.

"In here," I said, steamrolling into the only store around where an android wouldn't seem out of place if his hologram totally croaked.

Spencer's Gifts.

Home of the wacky, wild, weird, and wonderful. Masks. *X-Files* memorabilia. Aliens in snow globes. Aliens everywhere.

Erek shimmered. Shivered.

"Quick, into the corner," I said, nodding toward the back of the store, far away from the teenage guy running the register. "By the strobe lights. If anyone sees him, they'll just think his hologram's an optical illusion or something."

"Good idea," Cassie said, tugging at Erek's arm. "I wouldn't have thought of Spencer's."

"Mall knowledge," I said. "It's going to be my major in college."

Erek had stopped walking. He didn't move. Frowned. Steel and ivory plates flashed.

"Sorry," he apologized.

It was bizarre. Watching him was like wearing X-ray glasses and being able to see his bones right through his skin.

"Come on," I ground out.

He moved his leg. *Sloooowly.*

"Erek, please," Cassie whispered. "You have to hurry!"

"Oh, really?" he said, taking another slow-

14

motion step. "You know, the seriousness of the situation had totally escaped me."

"You can't walk, but you can be sarcastic?" Cassie demanded.

Then Erek froze stiff.

Cassie and I looked at each other. She took one arm. I took the other.

Somehow we hauled him down the aisle to the back of the store without anybody noticing us, but it was not easy. Erek was a hundred pounds or more of concrete. We propped him up in the corner between a stack of *Star Wars* posters and a life-sized replica of the alien from the movie *Alien*.

We stepped back.

The strobe light flashed.

Erek.

Android.

Erek.

Android.

Android.

Android.

"Oh, man," I muttered, glancing at Cassie.

"Now what?" she said.

I had no idea.

"Whoa, cool." It was some kid wearing a Hanson shirt. He slouched up and gazed at Erek's android form. "I wonder how much it is?" He moved in closer, searching for a price tag.

"Uhhh . . ." Cassie said helpfully.

"I'll find out," I said. "I mean, we want to know, too. Androids. They're cool." I backed away, motioning for Cassie to stay and keep an eye on poor Erek.

I had to do something to ward off shoppers, and fast. Fortunately, I knew how. I plucked the sales tag off a windup cockroach and slipped back into the aisle with the rubber-earthworm pens.

The cockroach had been five dollars. I crossed out the price, flipped the tag over, and scribbled "$5,000.00."

Hanson shirt said, "Five grand for a lousy hunk of metal that doesn't even walk or talk! What are they, nuts?" He took off. But someone else was sure to come along. And eventually the clerk, a nerdy college-age kid talking on the phone, was sure to notice.

When the kid was gone, Erek said, "Actually, my approximate value in current U.S. dollars would be well into the billions."

"Listen, stay here and guard him, okay?" I whispered to Cassie. "I'll be right back. And Erek? Don't worry, my friend, we'll get you out of here."

"Guard him?" Cassie said. "What do you mean, guard him? Wait!" She grabbed my arm. "You're gonna call Jake, right?"

"Think I should?" I said, a little giddy from having pulled it off so far. "I was thinking of calling for a pizza, but I guess I could call Jake instead."

Cassie gave me a sour look. "Thanks. Very funny. Here's a comic question for you: What do I do if some Controller sees Erek and realizes what he is?"

That wiped away some of my giddiness.

"Protect yourself," I said. I met Erek's frozen gaze. "You're number one, Cassie. Push comes to shove, give up Erek."

CHAPTER 4

I found a pay phone that wasn't being used. I punched in Jake's number and waited while it rang.

Be home, I thought, chewing on my bottom lip.

Four. Five. Six.

"Hello?"

"Jake?" I blurted, clutching the receiver.

"No, this is Tom."

I froze.

Tom, Jake's older brother. My cousin.

A Controller.

And the last person I wanted to talk to. I had to be careful. Very careful.

"Hi, Tom," I said casually. "It's Rachel. Is Jake around?"

"Yeah. Hold on." The receiver clunked down.

Hurry, I thought, glancing back at Spencer's. A group of three girls was heading in.

"Hello?"

"Jake!" I shouted into the phone. "Where the . . . where are you?"

"Huh?" he said, sounding confused.

Okay, Rachel, careful now. Just in case anyone is listening.

"I can't believe you forgot," I said, lowering my voice but trying to sound annoyed. "You were supposed to meet me and Cassie at the mall a half hour ago. We've been waiting in front of Spencer's for you."

A heartbeat of silence.

"Oh, man, sorry," Jake said, like he knew what I was talking about. "I was shooting hoops with Marco —"

"Good," I interrupted. "Bring him along. We ran into Erek, but we still need help carrying our packages home. They're very heavy. Very, *very* heavy."

"Yeah, okay," he said easily. "We're on our way."

"See ya!" I chirped cheerfully. I hung up. I forced a grin at some woman who was standing behind me waiting for the phone. I said, "Guys. Totally unreliable."

I took a couple of deep breaths. Now for the rest of it.

My first stop, The Gap.

There was only one way we were gonna be able to get Erek out of the mall, and that was the way he'd come in.

Through the door, as a human.

I put my credit cards through some serious exercise and went rushing back to Spencer's. I'd been gone for twenty minutes. I got back to find Cassie standing before a small group of kids and adults, including the Spencer's clerk.

Cassie was lecturing them. She was also sweating and breathing hard. Cassie is not a "look-at-me" kind of person.

"Yes, it's the latest thing from K-Tel. It's the all-new Kitchen Droid. It slices. It dices. It can make Julie Ann's fries."

"You mean julienne fries?" a woman asked skeptically.

"Anyone's fries," Cassie said, her voice tinged with desperation. "This Kitchen Droid will even ask, 'Do you want fries with that?'"

"So why isn't it doing all that stuff?" some kid asked.

"Yeah, turn it on," another said.

I saw Cassie's knees do a little wobble. She's definitely not a public speaker.

"This is just a mock-up, right?" I said loudly.

"Yes!" Cassie cried, as if I'd just told her the secret to winning the lottery. "Yes! This is just a mock-up! This isn't the actual Kitchen Droid! The *actual* thing won't be available till . . . oh, around, like, um . . ."

"In six months," I said.

The crowd dispersed. Cassie grabbed my arm and dug in her fingernails. "Where have you been? I've been sweating blood!"

"Shopping," I said. And before Cassie could strangle me, I added, "For Erek. He needs clothes and a disguise."

I started yanking a shirt and pants and underwear from the bags.

"Underwear?" Cassie shrilled. She held up a pair. "Tommy Hilfiger underwear? He's an —" She looked around to make sure no one could hear. "He's an android. He doesn't need designer underwear."

"Sorry. They don't have a Wal-Mart at the mall," I hissed.

"Uh, Rachel? He's an android? Excuse me? He doesn't even need pants, except as a disguise."

"Oh. Point taken." I looked at the briefs. "Maybe I'll give them to Jake."

"Excuse me?" Erek said. "Can we not discuss what —" He shut up suddenly.

"I just called my manager."

The voice made me jump. I spun around. The clerk.

"I just called my manager," he repeated. "He said there's no such thing as a Kitchen Droid. He wants me to find out who you are and call mall security and —"

"Grrrooooahhh!!"

The clerk jumped approximately six inches straight up.

"Oh, look! It's a guy in a gorilla suit," I said, almost laughing as I spotted Jake and a huge, hairy gorilla — an actual gorilla, of course — swaggering into the store.

The gorilla — Marco in morph — was wearing a sandwich board sign. It was crudely done in Magic Marker. It was an advertisement for a movie: *King Kong vs. Gudzilla*.

Yes, Gudzilla.

"That's a really realistic gorilla suit," the clerk said suspiciously.

"Look out!" I yelled at the clerk. "That Lava lamp is about to fall on your head and knock you out!"

"Huh?" He looked up and Marco totally missed his cue.

"I said, it's about to knock you out!" I repeated, glaring pointedly at Marco.

<Oh. Sorry,> Marco said in thought-speak. He reached out one canned-ham fist and gently tapped the clerk on the head. The clerk went down like a sack of wet cement.

"What's going on?" Jake demanded, once we were sure the clerk was still breathing.

"It's Erek. He's frozen up," I said. "I have clothes for him. Let's dress him, fast! And get him outta here."

"It's like the Tin Man in *The Wizard of Oz*," Cassie said, adjusting the poor clerk's position so he'd be comfortable in his unconsciousness. "You know, all frozen up."

"Let's get clothes on him," Jake snapped, taking charge.

It made me a little resentful. Also relieved.

"Marco, pick him up," Jake said.

Marco grabbed Erek around the waist and, using his tremendous gorilla strength, shoved arms into sleeves.

<Underwear?> Marco said. <You bought him designer underwear? Excuse me, he's an android!>

"We've gone through that, okay?" Erek said. "How about his face? A mask?"

Jake ran to snatch up some full-head masks.

"I have Clinton, Gingrich, and a Teletubby. Dipsy, I think."

"That's not Dipsy," Cassie corrected. "That's Tinky Winky. Dipsy's green and has the straight up thing. Tinky Winky's the one with the triangle."

<Who's the little red one?> Marco wondered.

"Po," Cassie said.

<Oh, yeah.>

"No offense," Erek said, "but how on Earth have you people managed to avoid getting caught for this long?"

Meanwhile, as this slightly idiotic conversation was going on, I was dressing my first android. I had guessed right on every size.

"I am the goddess of shopping," I said, feeling satisfied.

The clerk groaned.

"We need to hurry," Jake said. "Pick a face: Gingrich or Clinton?"

A minute later a gorilla wearing a sandwich board sign for a misspelled movie carried a very trendily dressed Bill Clinton over his shoulder out of the mall.

Fortunately, there was a big sale on at the department store, so not that many people noticed.

At least, that was my explanation then.

CHAPTER 5

We caught a bus to Erek's neighborhood and climbed down, feeling lucky. Feeling way too lucky.

"Good thing there was nobody on that bus but us," Jake said to me.

Marco was further ahead, loping down the sidewalk with Erek over his shoulder.

"Yeah." I looked around the quiet, deserted street. "Good thing. What're the odds of a gorilla carrying Bill Clinton going unnoticed? We walk out of the mall and no rent-a-cop tries to stop us? We take a bus and the driver barely notices? And we're the only passengers? I mean, come on. How likely is that?"

"Not likely," Cassie admitted.

"So Erek's exposed for an android but now that he's out of the mall, nobody's around to notice," I said. "Weird."

"Maybe it's not," Cassie said. "Maybe everybody's just busy and we're all just getting a little too paranoid, you know?"

Maybe, but I didn't think so. My gut instincts were telling me that there was something else going on here.

See, I've learned not to trust coincidences.

"You know what?" Jake said grimly. "When Marco and I got to the mall, there were electricians' trucks all over the place. I heard one of the workers say something about all the surveillance cameras going dead. I didn't worry about it then . . ."

What? No video record of anything that had happened, when the mall was probably crawling with Controllers? When a dressing room in The Gap was one of the main entrances to the Yeerk pool?

Not a chance.

"Yeerks?" Jake wondered with a frown.

"Why expose Erek and then make sure there's no proof?" I said.

"Are we being protected or set up?" Cassie asked.

"So is this some kind of, I don't know, like some weird safe passage, or what?" Jake mused.

"'Or what,'" I muttered.

<Would you mind speeding it up a little?> Marco called. <I've got about fifteen minutes left before I'm eating bananas and dragging my knuckles forever.>

"So basically no change from your usual self?" I called, then wished I hadn't.

See, morphing is an incredible weapon. But it's also a double-edged sword, because if you stay in a morph longer than two hours, you're trapped there forever.

Like Tobias.

Thinking of Tobias brought back all the morning's confusion.

Me, trying to be normal. Falling off the balance beam.

T. T., asking me out.

I was coming down off the adrenaline high. Normal emotions were resurfacing. Normal emotions like guilt. Guilt for even considering T. T.'s offer.

And as if he'd read my mind, Tobias swooped down and landed in a tree a few houses down on Erek's front lawn.

<What's going on?> he asked. <I just spotted you guys getting off the bus. Some reason why Marco's giving Erek a piggyback ride?>

Jake moved within speaking range of Tobias. "Has anyone been following us?"

<No. You're clean. Want to tell me what is going on here?>

<Erek seems to have missed his scheduled maintenance,> Marco explained. <He's frozen up. I think it's the transmission.>

"What if this is all a setup to find the Chee?" Cassie asked.

<Nobody's been following you,> Tobias repeated. <Besides, why bother? If the Yeerks catch any one of us, they'll get all the answers they need very quickly.>

He was right. If the Yeerks ever made a Controller of one of us, all our secrets would be out there.

"I don't know," Cassie said, shaking her head. "I think you were right, Rachel. There's something weird about all this."

And the minute Jake opened Erek's front door and we stepped inside, I knew it was gonna get even weirder.

CHAPTER 6

Mr. King, Erek's "father," was sitting on the couch. He had a TV remote in one hand and a pretzel rod in the other.

He looked like any other father on any other lazy day.

Except that his human hologram was gone, so he was sitting there like some weird android parody of normalcy. And, of course, he was no more Erek's father than I was. He was just another nearly eternal android playing a role.

"So it's not just Erek," I said.

"No," Mr. King said, without moving. "All the Chee have been immobilized. Holographic emitters down. Motor centers down. Logic centers, speech synthesizers, and Chee-net all function-ing normally."

<Chee-net?> Marco asked.

"Inter-Chee communication," Erek said. "We've had our own Internet since the days when your ancestors were still drawing pictograms on pyra-mid walls."

<Yeah? Cool. AOL. Androids On-Line.>

"But why is this happening?" Jake said. "How?"

"We don't know," Mr. King said.

Marco placed Erek on the sofa and started to demorph. Within minutes, the gorilla had shrunk and its coarse, black hair had been sucked back into Marco's human skin.

"You must have some idea what could do this. I thought you guys were indestructible," Jake said. He sounded a little annoyed. Which was okay. I was annoyed, too. We were used to the Chee being so in control, so capable.

Plus, it just had not been a good morning so far.

"The ship," Erek said.

"The ship?"

"The Pemalite ship."

"The Pemalite ship?" Marco echoed. "What Pemalite ship?"

"The one we hid in a deep, ocean canyon thousands of years ago when we arrived on

Earth," Erek explained. "It should have been safe from intruders. The atmospheric pressure down there will crush a human to the size of a guinea pig."

"Uh, how deep is that?" I said.

"Fifteen thousand feet," Mr. King said.

Marco whistled. "Almost three miles down."

We all looked at him, surprised.

"Hey," he said, "I told you before, I don't sleep through all my classes."

"Our Chee-net connects through the ship's onboard computer," Mr. King said. "That would be the only way to disable our systems."

<So, what? Somebody found the ship and activated the controls?> Tobias mused, perched on top of the TV and preening his right-wing feathers. <That still doesn't tell us who or why.>

"Or what they hope to get out of it," I added.

"Or how to reverse it," Jake said. "Is it even reversible?"

"Yes, that part would be simple. But reaching the computer would be a very dangerous undertaking," Mr. King said.

"Being a paralyzed android isn't exactly safe," I pointed out. "Especially since someone obviously knows you're here and vulnerable."

"What about other Chee?" Cassie asked.

"All the same," Erek said. "All have lost holograms and lost the capacity to move. Most are safe, out of sight. But two are presently at high risk. The first works as a janitor in a nuclear research facility. When his hologram failed, he locked himself in the safe the facility uses to store radioactive material."

"At least that sounds secure," Jake suggested.

"Only until the shift changes," Mr. King said. "At ten o'clock each night, all areas of the facility are inspected before the night crew takes over. Whoever opens that safe is going to expose a highly advanced . . . and nonhuman . . . technology."

"If the Yeerks get hold of our technology —" Erek began.

"Don't even *think* it," Marco muttered.

"Are we supposed to get into the nuclear plant?" I asked.

"No," Mr. King said. "It's maximum security. You wouldn't be able to get the Chee out undetected."

"What about the other Chee you said was in a bad situation?" Jake asked calmly. Jake always sounds calmest when he's most worried.

"She's in more immediate danger," Mr. King said. "Her human name is Lourdes."

"She's been living the low-life," Erek said. "She's a homeless street person."

"A what? Why?" Cassie demanded.

"We need access to all levels of society to track Yeerk activity," Erek said. "And don't feel too bad. You have to remember that we Chee live many lives. In her previous human guise, Lourdes was a movie actress. Very successful."

"She's been sleeping in an abandoned building. Abandoned except that half the building is being used to store stolen goods. It's sort of run by a fence named Strake," Mr. King continued. "We suspect he's a Controller."

"A Controller who fences stolen goods?" I asked, half-laughing.

"Yes," Erek said. "It puts him in touch with a broad range of the criminal element."

"Wow," I said. "Not all glamour being an android, is it?"

"Tell me about it," Erek said. "I'm passing as a junior high school kid."

"Point taken. Where is this Lourdes person now?" I asked.

"She made it to a closet under the front stairs," Mr. King said. "There's a complication: We have information that the police are going to raid the place. The raid will occur in about twenty minutes and we're certain there's at least one human-Controller assigned to the SWAT team."

"Twenty minutes!" I nearly shrieked.

"Time is short," Mr. King said apologetically. "But you understand that we cannot ask you to help rescue this Chee. There is a high likelihood of your being hurt."

"There's a high likelihood of us getting hurt every minute of the day," Marco said, exasperated.

"Where?" Jake demanded.

Erek gave us the address.

"Landmarks," I said impatiently. "We'll be flying in."

"Tobias, get Ax and follow us," Jake rapped. "Now!"

I snatched open the door and Tobias bolted.

"The abandoned house backs the railroad tracks. It's brick, surrounded by condemned buildings and close to a junkyard," Mr. King said. "Be careful. It's a bad neighborhood."

"Yeah, we're real worried about being mugged," I said with a laugh.

"So let me get this straight," Marco said. "We have to rescue a paralyzed Chee from a stolen goods warehouse before the Controllers get her. Then we have to dive down to the bottom of the ocean, find the Pemalite ship, somehow get inside it and turn off the signal before ten o'clock tonight so the Yeerks don't get the Chee in the safe at the nuclear waste facility. Is that pretty much it? Or do we have to discover the Fountain of Youth and come up with a low-fat cookie that tastes as good as Mrs. Fields's, too?"

"Ticktock," I said with a grin. "Ticktock."

"You are mentally ill," Marco said.

"There's one more thing," Erek said. "The Pemalite ship's signal will have been picked up by orbiting Yeerk spacecraft. They may already be down there waiting for you."

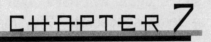

CHAPTER 7

<You know, if my father finds out I've been hanging around criminals, I'll be grounded for a year,> Marco joked as we flew toward the south side of town.

<You're not the only one,> I called back, careful to maintain my distance from the others, though staying close enough to communicate in thought-speak.

As we'd morphed, Erek had filled us in on accessing the Pemalite ship. Then we had bailed at top speed, pausing only long enough to change the channel on Erek's TV. The two Chee would be stuck there for a while.

We flew all out, forgetting about saving energy. We had energy. What we didn't have was time.

<Railroad tracks up ahead,> Jake said. <I wish Ax were here to keep track of time, if nothing else.>

Train tracks ahead. Along with junked cars, sagging buildings, and mounds of garbage. My eagle eyes showed me everything: the smashed liquor bottles, the empty vials. Spent bullet casings. Cigarette butts. Graffiti.

Even the air felt different here. Darker. Grayer.

Heavy with the absence of hope.

This battlefield had already been claimed by the enemy. And suddenly, I wasn't so sure we could take it back.

I was glad Ax wasn't there. I didn't want to have to explain this to him. And I doubted Tobias would find him in time to get involved.

Besides, who needed the extra firepower? Crooks might scare ordinary people, but not us. This was a quick, easy in and out. No biggie.

<That must be the place,> Jake said. <The house with the big steel door. Let's go!>

I spilled air from my wings, following him down into the bushy, overgrown backyard.

We had about five minutes left before the raid. Maybe. Not even enough time to land, demorph, and morph again.

These were bad odds, and yet . . .

The rush!

I landed in weeds and debris. I immediately began demorphing to human.

My beak rolled into my face. My head bulged and grew. My legs stretched, shooting me up into the air as my feathers dissolved and slithered back into my human skin.

I felt suddenly vulnerable. For the moment I was just a girl. A girl in a bad place. Time to morph again. Something big. Something dangerous. Something that didn't care too much about steel doors and nine millimeters.

Jake, Marco, and Cassie were beginning their own morphs. Jake was thinking like me: This was a bash job. Forget subtlety. The rhino horn was already growing from his forehead.

Marco's arms were long and covered with coarse, black hair. Cassie's face had elongated into a sleek, wolf's muzzle.

I hate being last. I closed my eyes and began my next morph in a hurry.

SPROOOOT!

My nose unraveled like a fire hose.

Morphing is never pretty. And it's never predictable. It happens in ways that don't quite kill you, but sometimes come pretty close. Things come popping out or disappearing in bizarre sequence.

That had just happened. I had a one-third

size elephant trunk sticking out of my otherwise normal face.

My bones ground and shifted, expanding until my head was big enough for the trunk — the size of one of those cute little Volkswagens.

My legs were thickening, huge as telephone poles. My skin darkened, toughened into leather.

Then, in one dizzying spurt, my tree stump legs became tree trunk legs. I shot straight up! Thirteen feet up into the air, as my body swelled into a muscled, fourteen-thousand-pound blimp.

I had good eyes and excellent ears the size of beach blankets.

Suddenly, the sound of car doors slamming. Wham. Wham. Wham.

"Police! Open the door!"

Glass shattering. Wood splintering.

Jake cursed. <The raid's started!> he yelled. <Marco, it's your job to snatch the Chee and get her out of there. The rest of us will cover you. Go! Go! Go!>

CHAPTER 8

"Down! Down!"

"Down on the floor! Hands behind your head!"

"I said down, don't move!"

There had to be a dozen cops, all yelling. How long before they found the Chee?

And if the cop who was a Controller found her first . . .

Heart pounding, I charged through brambles and bushes toward the house. The ground trembled beneath me. Literally.

Jake was at my side, keeping pace, following me because with rhino eyes he couldn't see well enough to know where he was going.

The back door opened and a filthy, skinny guy stumbled out.

"Eeeee-YEEEEE-uh!" I trumpeted.

"Ahhhh!" he screamed, turned, and ran back inside.

Then . . .

BLAM! BLAM! BLAM!

Gunfire!

<Me first, then you,> Jake said.

<Yeah,> I acknowledged.

WHAM! Jake slammed the back door and knocked it open, popping it loose from its hinges.

He backed up. I hit the doorway. I muscled shoulders into it, twisting and snapping the wood frame. Lifted up and buckled the ceiling. My huge head was inside, inside in the dark.

BLAM! BLAM! BLAM!

Bright gun flashes! Someone screamed. A dark shape rushed right in front of me. He was not wearing a uniform. I whipped my trunk and caught him in the belly.

We went down hard. The gun skittered from his fingers.

I pulled back and Marco and Cassie bounded through the hole Jake and I had made.

People were yelling. The air echoed with confusion.

"Freeze or I'll shoot! Hey! Is that a rhinoceros?!"

"Hhhhrrooooaaar!" Marco bellowed.

"Oh, man, I don't need a drink this bad!"

BLAM! BLAM!

A sharp, high-pitched yelp.

A wolf. Cassie.

Someone had shot Cassie!

Enraged, I put my shoulder against the back-door frame and pushed, this time with all I had. Bricks slid. Mortar crumbled. I pushed harder. The bricks buckled and the entire wall collapsed. Bricks thudded down around me, on me, but I hardly felt them.

"EEEEEYYEEE!" Trumpeting, I thundered through the wreckage. Dust clouded my vision. Clogged my lungs, making me sneeze.

"HA-CHOOO!"

The blast blew over a bony girl smoking a cigarette.

"Holy crap, an elephant!" someone shouted.

"Call for backup!" a cop shouted. "They got a whole circus in there!"

I swung my trunk, scattering a few rickety chairs. <Cassie?>

<Rachel?>

<Cassie? Where are you?> I called desperately, bashing through a wall and searching the

next room. The floor was lined with stained mattresses and reeked of stale pee and barf.

A chalk-skinned, blank-eyed guy, too stoned to even move, just lay there, staring up at me.

I picked him up by the ankle and tossed him out the hole in the wall. I didn't want to accidentally step on the guy. Let the cops deal with him later.

<I'm with Lourdes under the stairs,> Cassie cried. <Rachel, some jerk shot me in the back and I can't move my legs! I can't demorph with all these people around.>

A fierce, red bubble of anger popped deep inside my brain.

<Marco!> I shouted, ramming through another wall.

BLAM! BLAM! BLAM!

"Aaah! I'm hit!" a cop moaned from somewhere in the darkness.

<What?> Marco called back.

<Where's the creep with the gun?> I said, swinging my head and pulverizing the remains of a door frame.

<He's on the landing right above where Cassie's with that Chee. I can't get him. I've been stabbed. Not good. This place is a madhouse!> Marco yelled.

<They have me!> Jake reported from outside.

43

<I got lost and crashed out through the front and the cops have me surrounded with their patrol cars.>

This was insane! We were getting torn apart in the crossfire between the criminals and the cops.

First things first. The guy with the gun. The guy who'd shot Cassie.

I was mad. And I was big.

Nothing could stop me.

Wood, plaster, and paneling fell before me like confetti.

I was gutting the house.

I was on a rampage.

I headed for the rooms at the front.

Walls shook.

The rotted, wooden floor bowed, cracked, and gave way.

CRRREEEAAAKKK!

I stumbled, my legs dropping into the crawl space beneath the house. Four feet deep. Big deal. I got up and plowed through the sharp, splintered wood like a kid pushing through the surf at the beach.

Rusty nails and wood shards gouged my skin.

Pinpricks of pain. They didn't matter. I dug the floor up with my tusks.

The guy with the gun. I wanted him and I would have him.

And then, suddenly, there he was.

Crouched in front of the closet door under the stairs.

He was dirty. Skinny. Hollow-eyed.

He saw me, too.

Aimed his gun right at my head.

"Andalite," he sneered, and pulled the trigger.

CHAPTER 9

POW!

A sharp, stinging sensation. Searing, brutal pain.

Hot blood gushed from my head and blinded my right eye.

"EEEEEYYYEE-uh!" I swung my trunk like a baseball bat.

Felt it connect with his bony body.

UMPH!

"Aaarggh!" he howled, sailing across the room and crashing through the grimy, front window. He hit the ground and lay there, shattered glass raining down around him.

Through the awful pulsing in my head, I heard disembodied voices from the street.

"Hey, that's Strake! That's the guy we want. Quick, cuff him!" a cop shouted.

"What about this rhino? He's wrecking my squad car!"

"Somebody grab that gorilla before he rips the bar lights off my patrol car!"

"Don't worry about them right now! We've got Animal Control and some vet from The Gardens' wildlife park coming down. Let them deal with it! Just stay back!"

What? I blinked to clear my eye of seeping blood.

Some vet from The Gardens' wildlife park? I thought. Oh, great. Cassie's mother was the vet from The Gardens!

And she was mighty handy with a tranquilizer gun.

<Marco, can you get back in here?> I called, as a wave of weakness washed over me. <I've been shot.>

<I'll try, but now I've got about seven cops with shotguns pointed straight at my chest,> Marco said nervously.

"Tseeeeeer!"

"Geez, now a hawk, too?" a cop yelled. "What is this, *When Animals Attack*? Everybody hold your fire or we'll end up shooting each other!"

<Hurry up, Tobias, we're kind of in deep

here,> I called, squeezing my trunk around the closet door handle and yanking it open.

<I have Ax, too.>

That was the first good news I'd heard in a while.

An android sat propped against the dirty wall. A Chee.

A limp, panting wolf lay draped across her lap.

They were both drenched in blood.

<Lourdes?>

"Hi. You must be Rachel. Erek's told us all about you. Pleased to meet you."

<Uh, yeah, you, too,> I said, unsettled by the Chee's omniscience. Then, <Cassie, can you hear me?> I said.

The wolf lifted its head and gazed at me through dark, tormented eyes. <Yes.>

<Demorph. Do it now.> I said, wrapping my trunk around her and gently lifting her out of the closet.

<And get arrested?> She laughed weakly. <No way. My mother would kill me.>

"Get back! Run! Quick!"

Screams. Thuds. Pounding feet.

<Here, give her to me,> Marco said, appearing beside me and taking Cassie in his arms. Blood oozed from a large wound in his neck and

streaked his shoulder. Two nasty gashes ran down his right arm.

<What's going on out there?> I asked Marco, reaching back in and lifting Lourdes out of the closet with my trunk. Nothing to an elephant. Elephants can lift trees. An android was a feather.

<Jake got away. He's already around back.>

<How?>

<Tobias. He snatched some cop's gun and is flying around like psycho-bird, scaring everyone half to death. Even Strake is trying to crawl under a squad car.>

<Then let's do it,> I said.

<Now or never,> Marco agreed.

Stumbling, we turned in the tight space and came face-to-face with a cop. He was sweating, shaking. I couldn't blame him.

But his expression changed. I saw a new fear. And then, a familiar hatred.

"Andalites," he said.

Sneering, the cop raised his pistol and pulled the trigger.

BLAM! BLAM! BLAM! BLAM!

Cassie yelped.

Marco jerked, swayed, and pitched forward, disappearing down into the dark, dank crawl space.

CHAPTER 10

I blinked, too shocked to move.

The sharp, acrid scent of gunpowder filled the air.

The blast still rang in my ears.

"Give me the android, Andalite," the cop snarled.

I barely heard him.

Marco. Cassie.

I looked down into the crawl space.

They lay in a tangled, lifeless heap.

Their dark blood pooled and inched across the hard-packed dirt floor, spreading in an ever-widening circle toward my feet.

Thoughts skittered and blurred in my brain.

I was pinned. Trapped.

Backed up against the stairs to my right, Marco and Cassie to my left.

I was caught between their bodies below and the human-Controller cop poised on the creaky slope of flooring in front of me.

If I moved any way but forward, I'd crush Marco and Cassie.

But if I moved forward, I'd be dead.

<Marco? Cassie?> I shouted frantically.

Nothing.

If they were dead, this guy had killed them.

And now he was going to kill me and take Lourdes.

And the Yeerks would brutalize the Chee.

Grow stronger with their technology.

Become even harder to beat.

My muscles trembled and hate blackened my heart.

He'd killed my best friend.

He might even kill me. Fine. But he wouldn't get the Chee. Because I'd kill him first.

"Give me the android, Andalite," he repeated, raising his pistol and centering it on my already damaged forehead. He stepped forward, closing the gap between us to five feet.

<No. I don't think so,> I said.

I lifted my trunk, hoisting Lourdes high over my head. I hoped this nonviolent Chee warrior would forgive me for using her as a bludgeon.

"Give it to me and perhaps Visser Three will show you mercy!" he snapped. "You have no hope of escape," the cop continued, inching closer. "Your friends are dead and you're next."

I didn't want to die.

But better to die like a warrior.

A stark black-and-white blur caught the corner of my eye.

What?

Suddenly, a tiny, furry, helpless-looking creature about the size of a house cat came waddling in.

Harmless-looking, unless you knew what you were looking at. Unless you knew what that black-and-white striped tail meant.

The skunk — Ax, I assumed — darted between my huge feet, turned, aimed its butt at the Controller, and fired without warning.

The air filled with the thick, cloying stench of fresh, potent skunk.

You think you know what skunks smell like because you've smelled dead ones on the highway? You know nothing about the sheer, awesome power of that chemical weapon disguised as a cute fuzzy kitty.

"AAARGH!" the cop shrieked, clapping both hands over his eyes and falling back a step.

I almost fell with him. Ax hadn't hit me, but even a near miss is awful.

<Now, Rachel!> Ax commanded, scampering out of reach.

WHUMPF!

C-r-r-r-r-UNCH!

Flump!

My trunk, weighted with the android, slammed down on the Controller, buckling his knees and smashing him through the rotted floor to the crawl space below.

He twitched once and lay still. He was still breathing. I wasn't sure if I was glad about that.

Tobias swept in through the shattered front window and pulled up sharply. <Rachel, the Animal Control van just pulled up out front! Cassie's mother's with them and they have dart guns! We've got to get out of here!>

<I have to get Marco and Cassie,> I said, laying Lourdes on a hunk of stable flooring and dipping my trunk down into the crawl space.

<Your head wound is bleeding profusely, Rachel,> Ax said. <You must demorph before you become too weak.>

<In a minute,> I said stubbornly, fishing around in the darkness until I located one of Marco's hairy gorilla legs. I curled my trunk around it and hauled him up and out of the crawl space.

He hung upside down from my trunk, his arms swinging slowly, his body battered and matted with blood and dirt.

And then he opened his eyes.

<Stop the ride,> he said weakly. <I want to get off.>

<Marco!> I shouted, so startled that I almost dropped him. <I thought you were dead!>

<Yeah, well, sorry to disappoint you,> he mumbled.

The ground around us trembled. Chunks of plaster rained down from the ceiling and hairline fractures webbed what was left of the walls.

<I'll go out and distract Animal Control,> Tobias said, skimming back through the broken front window.

<Hurry, Rachel,> Ax warned as he waddled toward the front door. <I believe this building is unstable.>

I swung Marco up over my head and dropped him on my broad, leathery back.

<Can you hold on up there?> I asked. <At least until we get out to the railroad tracks?>

<Can King Kong climb the Empire State Building?> he retorted, grabbing handfuls of the thin, wiry hair on my head and gripping me with his knees.

Again I reached into the crawl space and curled my trunk around Cassie's limp wolf body.

It was still warm. Her heart was beating beneath her fur.

I went weak with relief.

<Grab her,> I said. I held her up, my knees trembling, until Marco pulled her into his lap.

I reached back down for Lourdes. I could hardly see. One of my eyes was blinded by blood. The other was strangely blurred. I swung the android up onto my back.

<Head for the nearest circus,> Marco said.

We bailed.

CHAPTER 11

<The heck with running for the railroad tracks,> I yelled, plowing a swath through the floor toward the front door. <Hang on tight, guys, because we're outta here!>

I lifted my trunk and blasted a high, enraged scream.

Then I barreled through the doorway, tearing out an elephant-sized chunk of wall.

WHUMPF! CRRRACK!

"Whoa! Get out of the way! Move it!"

"Back off, people! I need a clear shot! Back off!"

Chaos. People darting everywhere.

Tobias, still dive-bombing with a gun in his

talons, was trying to keep Cassie's mom from getting a clear shot with her dart gun.

Pop!

<Cassie, your mommy is shooting at us,> I said.

I caught sight of Ax, planted squarely in the middle of the sidewalk, and scooped him up with my trunk as I thundered through the milling crowd.

<I believe this animal's defense mechanism will assist us in escaping,> Ax said, lifting his tail.

<Go for it,> I said, surging forward and holding Ax out like a weapon.

"Skunk! Oh, no! It's spraying! Get out of the way!"

The mob parted. I heard them shouting, saw their panicked bodies hurtling aside as I rocketed past.

CCCRRREEEAK!

<The warehouse is coming down!> Tobias yelled.

<I'm not surprised,> I called back, charging down the street. I spotted Jake up ahead and followed him. <Where are we going?>

<I don't know!> he cried. <I'm half blind!>

<I suggest you split up,> Lourdes said. <There's a junkyard ahead on the left and an abandoned parking deck on the right.>

<I'll scout them,> Tobias said, flapping hard for altitude.

<Uh, Rachel?> Marco said. <You're gonna have to pull over soon. I'm not as okay as I thought I was. Lourdes is slipping.>

<What about Cassie?> I said anxiously, blinking in a futile effort to clear my eyes.

<Her eyelids are twitching. I think she might be coming around,> Marco said breathlessly.

The sound of sirens filled the air. Tires squealed as the cops gave chase.

<Swerve right, Jake. I'll guide you into the parking deck,> Tobias called.

"Turn left, Rachel," Lourdes said. "Follow the dead-end street to the junkyard. I can be hidden there until the signal from the Pemalite ship is turned off."

<You know about that?> I gasped as I stumbled over a broken slab of asphalt. <Never mind, I forgot: Chee-net.>

<Rachel?> Cassie called weakly.

<Demorph, Cassie,> I cried, barreling desperately down the deserted street and up to the junkyard's padlocked metal gates.

I held Ax safely out of the way under my front legs and, pressing my bleeding head against the gates, pushed until the lock sprung open.

My head didn't hurt anymore. Nothing hurt.

I was swaying now. It surprised me when my front legs simply buckled. I hit hard, but I wasn't feeling much anymore when my tusks dug into dirt.

The Chee, Cassie, and Marco must have tumbled from my back. But I was too confused to know. Confused. Head spinning, eyes going dark.

Nothing made sense. I was sinking. Sinking into a deep, deep, soft bed and . . . and someone kept yelling, <Demorph, Rachel! Do it now!>

CHAPTER 12

We were a shaken-up bunch of animal-morphing freaks by the time we at last made it home. A situation that should have been a walk in the park had turned into a mess.

The Chee were grateful to us. Me, I was grateful that Tobias and Ax had shown up when they did.

I was definitely not in the best of moods. I was feeling brittle and tired and mad at the world. Maybe it was just one too many battles. Or maybe it was because I'd been thinking about what we had to do next.

Dive fifteen thousand feet down into the cold, dark ocean.

Deeper than we'd ever gone before.

Deeper than a dolphin or a hammerhead shark could dive.

Up against an enemy that couldn't be fought: the deadly, crushing pressure.

It worried me because I couldn't think of a way to beat it, and if we couldn't beat it, then it would beat us.

Crush us.

And all of it in a hurry. The time was counting down.

Ticktock.

We couldn't go to Cassie's barn. We couldn't risk her parents making her do anything. We were all looking at plenty of parental trouble, but we had no time. Better a week of being grounded compared to losing this battle.

We assembled in the woods near Tobias's meadow.

<Tobias has informed me of the situation,> Ax said. <And he says the atmospheric pressure is deadly at the depth we must travel.>

"It is for us, Ax-man," Marco said. "We'll be crushed like a beer can on a frat boy's forehead."

<Frat boy? What is a frat boy?> Ax wondered.

"Forget it," Marco said. "It was only a joke."

"Not really," I said.

<Ah. Human humor,> Ax replied, nodding.

"Not really," I repeated, giving Marco a look. I was teasing Marco. But the truth was, there was nothing funny about being crushed to death. The image of it bothered me. The feeling of being squeezed on every inch of my body, pushed inward, internal organs squishing and . . .

"I don't know how we're going to do this," I blurted. "None of our morphs are capable of diving that deep and without one, we're talking about a kamikaze mission, here."

<"Kamikaze"?> Ax asked.

"It means suicide, Ax," I said. "Death, to you and me."

"Saving the Chee isn't going to be a suicide mission," Jake said, glaring at me. "You're overreacting, Rachel."

My jaw dropped.

Worrying about something as lethal as atmospheric pressure was overreacting? Wanting to get home in one piece instead of dying a stifling, airless death on the dark ocean floor was overreacting?

Since when?

If Cassie had said it, Jake wouldn't have told her she was overreacting. He would have agreed. He would have thought she was being sensibly cautious.

Wasn't I allowed to be cautious?

No, of course not, I thought bitterly. *I'm supposed to be a reckless fighting machine and fighting machines don't feel caution or fear. And even if they do, they don't advertise it.*

"Well, excuse me, I guess I'll just shut up and follow orders," I said.

"Look, I'm sorry, Rachel," Jake said tiredly. "You made a good point in a bad way, okay? But nobody's gonna die because we're not gonna dive unless we find the right morph."

<Is there no Earth being that can dive down fifteen thousand feet?> Ax asked.

"I don't think so," Cassie said, frowning. "I mean, the only deep-sea creature that even comes close is a sperm whale, and their record is like ten or twelve thousand feet, I think."

<We could hijack a diving bell,> Tobias offered lamely. <You know, one of those little submarines?>

"Yeah, we could tell everyone we're going to find the *Titanic*," Marco said. "We could see if Leo DiCaprio is floating around down there. But what do we do if we get down there in a stolen sub? We still have to get inside this Pemalite ship."

"It was just an idea," I said, defending Tobias.

We each had at least one situation that still gave us nightmares. I had more than one. Sometimes they were all mixed up and fragmented, like shattered glass that just keeps on reflecting broken, jagged images.

And we each had morphs we'd hated.

Tobias's worst moments all dealt with water.

<Looks like a wet one,> Tobias said glumly. <I am so totally not interested in being Captain Nemo.>

"Hello!" Cassie cried suddenly. "That's it! *Voyage to the Bottom of the Sea!* Hah! I think we may have a solution!"

CHAPTER 13

"Wasn't it *Journey to the Bottom of the Sea*?" Marco asked.

"No, it was *Voyage*," Jake confirmed.

"Journey sounds better," Marco said.

Jake sighed. "Hey, time marches on, right? We're in a hurry. What are you thinking, Cassie?"

"Calamari," she said with a grin.

"Snails?" I said, frowning.

<I am not in favor of snails,> Ax said.

"Wait, that's not —" Cassie said loudly.

<I had the misfortune to inadvertently eat one while feeding,> Ax continued. <I did not see it in time. I stepped on it and digested it.>

"You ate a snail through your hoof?" I asked. That picture temporarily replaced the image of

65

me being squashed to the size of a Barbie doll on the ocean floor.

<Yes, and the meat portion was fine. However, once the snail's body had been digested, the shell was very difficult to —>

"Ooookay, I think that's probably enough about snails," Jake said.

"Yeah, especially since *calamari* does not mean snail," Cassie pointed out. "*Escargot* means snail. I was talking about —"

<I have an idea: Let's all just stick to speaking English,> Tobias grumped.

"Squid!" Cassie yelled suddenly. The birds in the trees around us fell silent. So did we.

Until Tobias said, <Uh-uh. *Calamari* is octopus, not squid.>

"Oh. Who. CARES?" Cassie cried. "Squid. We can morph a giant squid! Giant squid dive really deep. And they have arms, so we could maybe get into the Pemalite ship."

I met Marco's gaze. "Why didn't she just say that to begin with?"

"Could have saved a lot of time," Marco agreed, playing along.

<What does any of this have to do with your Captain Nemo?> Ax wondered.

Cassie threw up her hands. "It's a book. *Journey to —*"

"Ah HAH! It was *Journey*!"

"I mean *Voyage to the Bottom of the Sea*," Cassie grated. "Captain Nemo was attacked by a giant squid."

"Who won?" Marco asked.

"Wait a minute," I said. "It wasn't Journey or Voyage. It was *20,000 Leagues Under the Sea*. Jules Verne."

Cassie looked like she might strangle me. Then she said, "Oh yeah. *Voyage* was a TV show. They run it on the Sci-Fi channel."

"I thought it was on Nick at Night," Marco said.

At which point everyone started giggling.

"Someone call the Chee and tell them they're doomed," I said. "Their only hope is a collection of idiot kids, standing around in the woods debating cable channels."

"We are in a hurry," Jake said, tapping his wrist where a watch would be. "So? What about giant squid? Where do we find one to acquire?"

Cassie shook her head, suddenly glum. "I don't know. I hate to say this, but I'm pretty sure there aren't any in captivity."

"Well, then that's not very helpful, is it?" Marco said.

Cassie shrugged. "No. And it's not like we can go dolphin and find one. The only thing that eats giant squid is the sperm whale."

Pretending to be more nonchalant than I felt,

I said, "Okay, so we acquire a sperm whale, dive down, and grab us a big squid."

Cassie shook her head. "No sperm whales in captivity. There never have been."

"There has to be a way," Jake said. But he sounded doubtful. "Anyone have any suggestions?"

No one did.

"You're kidding," I said. "That's it? We're beat?"

"We have till ten P.M.," Jake said. "What's that? Eight hours? Not exactly enough time to go whale hunting. Cassie?"

She held up her hands, helpless. "That was my one idea: squid. The Pemalite ship is just too far down."

"And time is too short," I said.

"The alternative is trying to bust into that nuclear facility and get the Chee out. The safe is too strong for us. And one other huge problem: The guards there are normal humans, as far as we know," Jake said. "We can't exactly go busting in and just kick everyone's butt."

"Anyway, that only solves the problem of that one Chee," Marco pointed out. "What about the others? We can't just leave them sitting around as stiff as lawn ornaments."

But in the end, it looked like that was our only

choice. We broke up and headed home with no hope.

It was depressing. I mean, we'd messed up missions before, but we'd never been lame enough to fail before we'd even started.

Now the Chee would be lost and the Yeerks would possess technology that would stump even Ax.

Atmospheric pressure, our own Earth force, had beaten us.

Cassie headed toward her farm. Jake and Marco headed to Erek's to tell him the bad news.

Tobias and Ax melted back into the woods.

I walked home alone.

CHAPTER 14

My neighborhood looked normal.

Kids playing street hockey. Adults sweeping driveways.

Gossiping about the gorilla who'd been at the mall.

"And by the time the news van arrived, the gorilla was already gone," one woman said.

"Someone said they saw him abduct a child," the other woman said nervously. "I'm afraid to let my kids out of my sight."

I kept my face carefully blank as I passed, but inside my heart was pounding. A news van had shown up? Had they found out anything? Had they tracked our movements somehow?

Were Jake and Marco walking into an ambush at Erek's?

I started to jog, then to run. I bolted across my front lawn and into the house.

"I'm home," I yelled, slamming the door behind me.

"I was beginning to think you'd been abducted by this so-called gorilla haunting the mall," my mother called. "And now on the news there's something about an elephant at a flophouse."

"Yeah? Elephants with drug problems?" I said, entering the kitchen.

My mother had half the table covered in legal papers. The other half was set for dinner.

I grabbed the phone and dialed Jake's house. Let it ring thirteen times. Hung up.

Called Marco. Got his answering machine and hung up.

What now?

"Did you hear about the gorilla who was riding an elephant into some abandoned house?" my sister Jordan asked, switching on the TV.

"Shut it off, Jordan," my little sister Sara whined. "You know we don't watch TV while we eat."

"But they're gonna show the gorilla on the news," Jordan said, blocking the TV so Sara couldn't touch it. "Mom!"

"Sara, watching TV this once won't hurt anything. Now, sit down and eat," my mother said absently, shuffling through her papers. "This is the last weekend I have to prepare this case and I'd appreciate your cooperation."

"Yeah," Jordan said, smirking at Sara.

"You're ugly when you do that," Sara said.

"Look, here's the story," I interrupted, pointing at the TV as the familiar front of the mall covered the screen.

"In local news, a publicity-seeking gorilla kicked up quite a stir at a mall today," the anchorman announced. "Some say the primate was an actor promoting a soon-to-be-released movie. Others, however, insist it was a real gorilla."

The camera flashed to the sales kid at Spencer's Gifts.

I caught my breath.

"Sure I saw it," the kid said, shrugging. "It was just some guy in a gorilla suit. No big deal. But he dropped a lava lamp on my head."

"What about the rumors that it had abducted a child?" the reporter asked solemnly.

The kid laughed. "Look, we get all kinds in here, like folks into alien abductions. We get a lot of college kids, too."

"So you think this was a fraternity prank?" the reporter asked.

The kid shrugged again. "Probably."

The camera flashed back to the studio. "Adding to this mystery is that all of the security cameras malfunctioned while the gorilla was in the mall, so there is no videotape for police to review. However, there have been no reports filed in connection with any missing children. And police deny reports that a bust at a stolen goods warehouse turned up a small zoo full of exotic animals."

"Man, I'm never around when the good stuff happens," Jordan complained, plopping down at the table. "Burritos. Yum."

My stomach growled and I started eating. I snagged two volumes of our ten-year-old encyclopedia and started reading as I ate.

The volumes covered the "Sq" and "Wh" entries: squid and whale.

So there really was no videotape. Good. No problem.

But wait. We'd taken a bus home. What about the bus driver?

If the Yeerks got him, they'd tap into his memories and know exactly who we were and where we'd gotten off the bus.

I shut the encyclopedia. And I almost missed the next news story.

"The entire town is trying to save a fifty-nine-foot whale that beached itself on the coastline less than fifteen minutes ago," the anchorwoman chirped. "This is the first marine mammal stranding in the town's history. Let's go live to the scene."

The burrito lodged in my throat. I swallowed hard.

The reporter was standing on the beach.

And behind him was a massive, wrinkled wall of whale.

I didn't hear much of what the reporter was saying.

Something about volunteers and the whale surviving.

"What kind of whale is that?" I croaked.

My mother glanced up from her paperwork. "Hmmm? Oh, they just said it was a sperm whale."

And then the camera zoomed in, and suddenly the whale and I were looking straight at each other.

His dark, solemn gaze locked onto mine.

I pushed back my chair.

This was no coincidence.

Someone or something wanted us out there bad. And was willing to sacrifice a whale to do it.

"Aren't you going to finish your dinner?" my mother asked as I grabbed the phone.

"I'm not hungry," I said, punching in Cassie's number.

"Hi," I said, when she answered. "What're you doing?"

"I just came in from the barn," she said. "Why?"

I chose my words carefully. We never trust phones. "Well, we were just watching the news and they had some bizarre stories about a gorilla tearing through the mall and a sperm whale beached down at the shore. Weird, huh? How come we always miss all the interesting stuff?"

"A sperm whale," she said slowly. "Uh-huh. Well, it's a shame, but there's nothing we can do about it. We already have plans for tonight."

"Oh, yeah, I know," I said and then, in case anybody was listening, added, "you're gonna learn how to cartwheel if it's the last thing I do."

She laughed. "Sure. See ya."

I hung up and yelled that I was going to Cassie's.

My mother barely looked up from her paper-work.

Sometimes having a busy mom is a good thing.

I walked out into the evening, steaming. Someone was playing games with us. Someone was treating us like a bunch of sock puppets. Jerking us around.

I was mad. But it was a cold anger. A calm, cold anger.

We'd see who jerked who.

CHAPTER 15

I went around the back of the house and slid into the shadows between the hedges and the fence. Pulled off my running shoes, jacket, and jeans. Concentrated on my bald eagle morph.

Instantly I felt the changes begin.

I was falling like an elevator with a snapped cable.

My bones crunched, hollowing out and re-molding themselves.

SPPPRRROOOUT! Wings burst from my back.

My face shifted and bulged. My chin slid away and my nose stretched, hardening into a fierce, deadly beak.

Feathers etched a tattoo pattern on my skin,

then rose and formed dappled layers. My vision sharpened.

The eagle's brain wanted to hunt. It wanted to eat.

Get a grip, Rachel. Think about what you have to do.

And suddenly, my mind was clear.

I spread my wings and took off.

First, I had to get to Erek's to make sure Marco and Jake hadn't walked into an ambush. Just because the news hadn't mentioned our bus driver didn't mean the Yeerks hadn't found and questioned him.

Aha! Down below, Marco and Jake stepped out of Erek's and closed the door.

<Hey, guys, it's me,> I called, dipping a wing when they glanced up. <Listen, a live sperm whale washed up on the beach. We have to acquire it. Be at Cassie's as soon as possible.>

I knew they couldn't answer me in thought-speak, so I drifted above them for a few minutes, watching for a sign.

And I got one, as soon as Jake turned down one street and Marco turned down a different one.

<Okay, Jake, you have to go home first?> I asked.

He nodded and walked faster. Broke into a

jog. Marco was morphing behind someone's shed.

I flew as fast as I could to Tobias's meadow. He saw me coming and listened as I told him about the whale.

<I'll get Ax,> he said. <You know, this is bull, Rachel. We need a sperm whale and all of a sudden we have one? I don't think so.>

I veered off and headed back toward the barn. Cassie was perched in a wild cherry tree waiting for me, already morphed to osprey.

Marco, in osprey morph, landed nearby. <Gee, can we all spell "coincidence"?>

<Somebody wants us to get to that Pemalite ship,> I said.

<Or die trying,> Marco added grimly.

A red-tailed hawk and a northern harrier drifted into view.

<Where is Prince Jake?> Ax asked.

<He had to stop home first,> Marco replied. <His parents were expecting him. He has to weasel out somehow.>

Jake showed up twenty minutes later. <You'll all appreciate this little update: The Sharing is sending volunteers down to help save the whale. You know, what with TV cameras being there. Gives them a great opportunity to be saintly and environmental and all.>

So the place was going to be crawling with Controllers.

<Maybe that's it, maybe not,> Cassie said. <They may think it's one of us.>

<We're being manipulated here,> Jake said. <But not by the Yeerks. Not even they can arrange for a sperm whale to conveniently beach itself. They could shoot one, but talk a live one into beaching? Not their style.>

<So who? Who goes to all the trouble to get to the Pemalite ship, use it to mess with the Chee, and then hand us the means to get down there?> Tobias wondered. <Not the Yeerks. Not the Ellimist. Not his style. So who?>

<Or *what?*> Marco said.

<Come on, let's go,> Jake said. <Just everyone keep your eyes open. This whole thing stinks.>

<We may not have long,> Cassie said. <Beached whales can't support their weight on land. They end up crushing themselves to death. That whale is slowly suffocating.>

I felt a shiver of fear. Suffocating. The whale was suffocating.

A whale, beached so we could acquire it. A pawn in someone's game. Expendable.

Not if I could help it.

<Let's do it,> I said.

CHAPTER 16

It wasn't a long flight in a straight line. But we couldn't fly in a straight line. We'd have been a whole sky full of raptors flying in formation. Slightly conspicuous.

So we stayed far apart at different altitudes, never seeming to go in the same direction at all.

It took a while to reach the beach. It was empty of sunbathers. The sun was weak and watery and heading down. Besides, what people were still at the beach were gathered around to gape at the spectacle.

It lay below us, improbable, out of place. Huge. It dwarfed the small army of humans who clustered around it like busy ants around road-kill.

The whale looked dead. But I knew it wasn't. Whoever or whatever was directing this little play wouldn't allow it to be dead.

<Erek didn't believe us when we said we couldn't find a way to get to his ship,> Jake said. <He said, "You will. We have faith in you.">

<Wow. And I thought the Chee were so smart,> Marco said. <I mean, Erek's spent time with us. You think he'd know better than to trust us.>

That got a laugh from everyone. The time Erek had spent with us had involved a trip to the planet of the Iskoort, and a deadly confrontation with a creature of infinite power and malice: the monster called Crayak.

<I think it's inspiring,> Cassie said.

<Well, then, you'll love what else Erek told us,> Marco called. <Since the Pemalites considered everyone a friend, their ship's adapted to accommodate different life-forms. You touch one of the interface panels throughout the ship, your life-form is analyzed, and the ship provides you with the correct environment.>

<How do we get in and shut off the signal?> I said, heading for a deserted dune far away from the crowd around the whale.

<Mr. King gave us an access code that'll get us into the main computer,> Jake said, his tone sardonic. <Everybody memorize it: Six.>

<Six?> I said.

<Six,> he confirmed.

I sighed. <You know, I'm sure the Pemalites were wonderful people and all, but using a single-digit security code? I mean, good grief. What a bunch of idiots.>

<They trusted,> Cassie said simply.

<They're dead,> I said, just as simply.

We landed behind a dune in an area of tall scruffy grass. Tobias stayed airborne, always on alert.

This was going to be a little hairy. If anybody came over that dune and saw us, they'd run screaming all the way to the next county.

We were mutants. A group of bulging, stretching, pulsating blobs of feathers and flesh, fingers and wings. Stubby little people with beaks and talons, legs and hair.

The first thing I noticed when I was fully human again was the smell. The fresh smell of salt and sand. Birds of prey have hearing and sight that is far superior to humans. But they are not into smell or taste.

"It's occurred to everyone that this is all a trap, right?" I said.

"What?" Marco mocked. "You suspect treachery? Now, why didn't I think of that?"

I ignored him. "Okay, so look, we don't expose anyone we don't have to here."

Jake smiled at me. "You volunteering?"

I shrugged.

"Rachel's right," Marco said. "We go out there all together, we're exposed. How many of us do we need to morph whale?"

Jake nodded. "A couple, anyway. I'm not sending anyone squid-hunting without backup. But you're both right. The less exposure, the better. So we pick two of us to acquire the whale. Excluding Ax, who can't because he'd have to be in his own body to acquire."

"And that might cause some slight disruption down on the beach," I said.

"Two of us will morph into whales and go find a squid," Jake continued. "The rest of us will use our dolphin morphs, stay topside as backup —"

"Who gets to be the whales?" I interrupted. "I'll go."

Cassie rolled her eyes. "You know, Rachel, you're like the smart kid in class who sits in the front and always raises her hand. 'I know! I know!' Only with you it's 'I'll go! I'll go!'"

I laughed at the image.

"I guess we'll draw straws," Jake said. He bent down and yanked up some grass and began breaking the stems into pieces.

<Ahh. The human scientific method,> Ax said.

As usual with Ax, it was hard to tell if that was supposed to be a joke.

Jake put his hands behind his back, then held them out in his fist. "Pick. Short ones are whales."

Part of me wanted to hang back. I had bad mental images of the world several miles underwater. But most of me wanted to go, and for the same reason: because it scared me.

Tobias landed on a broken piece of wooden fence. <I'm in on this,> he said.

I met his fierce gaze. I looked hard at him, as hard as he looked at me.

<No,> he said in thought-speak only I could hear.

I narrowed my eyes and pressed my lips tight together. I couldn't thought-speak, but Tobias would get the message.

<Rachel, no,> he said. <I am not going to help you get yourself killed.>

Marco drew a straw. A long one.

Cassie drew. Long straw.

I glared at Tobias.

<Okay fine,> he snapped in angry surrender. <The second from your left.>

I pulled the straw second from the left. "Short," I announced, holding it up.

<My turn,> Tobias said.

Jake walked over to him and held out his hand. Tobias pecked up a straw with his beak.

<Short,> he said, looking hard at me.

"Rachel and Tobias," Jake said, letting the other straws fall. He looked from Tobias to me, suspicious.

I shot Tobias a furious stare. He hated the water! He could never entirely subdue his hawk instincts, instincts that told him water was definitely not his environment. It scared him. But he'd cheated to pick the short straw for himself.

My fault. I'd insisted on going. Tobias wasn't going to let me go down there without him to watch my back.

Later, I would be kind of touched by that loyal gesture. But right then I was just mad: Tobias was risking his own life because I was jerk enough to make him cheat for me.

Guilt. I hate guilt.

Jake sighed heavily. "All right. Rachel? You and Cassie go down to save the whale. Cassie being there will seem normal. Everyone knows she's —"

"— a tree-hugging animal nut," Marco interjected.

"And everyone knows Rachel is Cassie's best friend. It works out. Tobias? In and out, man. Choose your time, zip in, lock talon, and bail.

The rest of us will stay up here as backup. Ax? Morph to seagull and give us some air cover."

Cassie and I started down the dune. Jake grabbed my arm and pulled me aside for a private word. "Don't you ever do that again," he said, far angrier than I'd suspected. "It's your fault Tobias is going. Remember that next time you decide to make fools of the rest of us."

He let me go and I walked away, a little shaken. Jake doesn't get mad much. When he does, it sticks in your mind.

"Coming, Rach?" Cassie called, already down the dune.

Oh, yeah.

This party couldn't start without me.

CHAPTER 17

A x merged with the gulls screaming and wheeling overhead.

<Stay away from the front of the bucket brigade,> Tobias called down. <Chapman's there, and so is Tom.>

"They must be expecting something to happen," Cassie said.

"Well, they're right," I said.

"Look," Cassie whispered, going still.

I came up behind her and followed her stricken gaze.

Felt my stomach drop.

The whale was a toppled skyscraper. A huge eighteen-wheeler, one of the big rigs. A string of railroad cars.

A gigantic, tragic, breathing, out-of-place mistake.

It didn't belong on land. But it was here, and helpless. Slowly being crushed by its own mass.

"Oh, no," I said softly as it feebly moved a flipper. All that immense power and it couldn't save itself.

I clenched my hands into fists. Dug my nails into my palms.

"I am going to hurt whoever did this," I whispered.

"I'll help," Cassie said.

I forced myself to look closely at the whale. Study it. Learn it. Its head was a huge, boxy rectangle that ran almost half of its total length. It had a blunt, squarish snout, a narrow, underslung jaw dug into the wet sand, and small, dark, glistening eyes.

I elbowed my way into a group of bucket-bearers near the water and someone thrust a bucket into my hands.

I emptied it over the whale's wrinkled side.

Another bucket, another pitifully small splash of water.

The whale's tail was still in the ocean and every few minutes it thrashed weakly and kicked up sandy waves.

Some guy, a biologist who was some kind of whale expert, yelled, "Hold up!"

The bucket line stopped as the man stepped in to draw blood into a large syringe.

I glanced quickly at the people next to me. I saw Cassie further down the line. She nodded very slightly.

I pressed my hand against the wall of gray flesh. Wet. Warm. Gritty with sand that had been picked up in the water.

I felt the calm descend on the whale. I absorbed its DNA into me, feeling presumptuous and small and silly somehow.

Then the biologist was done and we went back to work. Bucket after bucket. Several dozen humans working hard to save one whale. Failing, but trying anyway.

Every now and then I'm actually proud of my species.

<Prince Jake and Marco must relocate. Some humans have stopped near our previous location,> Ax said, his thought-speak voice startling me.

I glanced down the beach and spotted Jake and Marco, running and kicking at the surf. Playing the roles of carefree kids. They turned back toward the dunes.

What about Tobias? Had he acquired the whale yet? His was the biggest risk because he had to do it while in red-tailed hawk form. Hawks don't exactly hang out on beaches.

I had no answers, so I followed Jake's and Marco's footprints into the hollow, where three identical seagulls were waiting for me.

<Have you seen Tobias?> Marco asked, cocking his head.

"No," I said, concentrating hard on my own seagull morph.

<How about Cassie? Is she coming?> Jake asked.

"You know Cassie. You'll have to *tell* her to stop working down there."

Feathers sprouted. My nose dissolved and a beak began to push out. I was falling toward the sand, shrinking, as waist-high dune grass suddenly loomed tall above me. I spread my arms/wings to steady myself.

Hello!

An empty Lay's Barbecue Chips bag I hadn't noticed before. And at least two chips! All I had to do was hop on over and —

<Rachel. Deal,> Marco said.

Oh, yeah. This was not mealtime. Of course, to the seagull brain, it was always time for trash.

<Prince Jake, a situation has arisen,> Ax called down. <Tobias has been spotted and the Controllers are suspicious.>

<We're on our way!> Jake said, taking off.

We followed him, cresting the dune.

Tobias was perched on the whale's back.

Chapman stood below him, pointing and staring.

<Tobias! What are you doing?> I demanded.

<I'm stuck! My talon is caught on some kind of barnacle or something!>

<Diversion!> Jake snapped. <Now!>

<Make it look like we're chasing the hawk away from our territory,> Cassie said. <Try slamming Tobias. It may knock him loose.>

<Oh, great,> Tobias grumped.

We flapped hard and took off, not worried about flying together. We were seagulls. We belonged. Besides, we weren't the only gulls wheeling around the whale.

<Let's wreak some havoc,> I said.

I gained altitude, thirty or forty feet, and swooped. I snatched a man's pretzel right out of his mouth.

We milled and screeched; we stole food and sideswiped people; and we used the seagull's ultimate weapon: precision guided, cruise-missile poop.

<Chapman is mine,> Marco said. <Ready. Aim . . . hah!>

Sploot!

Chapman wasn't looking up. A pity.

I broke away from the melee and aimed for Tobias. <Which talon?> I asked.

<Oh, man,> he groaned. <Left.>

I hit him, chest out, barely braking. I caught him where his left leg met his own chest.

Whumpf!

The talon tore free. Tobias flapped, skimming along the back of the whale.

Zing!

A rock shot past, expertly thrown. It missed Tobias by a feather. I saw Tom stoop to find a second stone in the wash of surf. I saw hatred on his face.

CHAPTER 18

<That's just sad,> Tobias said. <Controllers reduced to throwing rocks. Hey, a couple of you need to chase me. You know, chase me away.>

We did.

Did Chapman and Tom buy the act? Probably not. They'd both seen a red-tailed hawk too many times before. They knew. But what could they do?

We followed the beach, out of sight of the whale's various saviors, then turned and headed out to sea. Tobias gained altitude, flapping hard with nothing but dead air to lift him. When he had altitude enough, he began to morph to seagull himself. He did it in midair.

We skimmed the gray, choppy waves until we

were sure we couldn't be seen from the beach. The light was fading. The sun was going down.

The ocean is always intimidating. But when the sun sets and darkness rolls across the waves, you just can't help but be awed and abashed and a little frightened of it.

Millions and millions of cubic miles of water. Twenty miles deep in places. Stretching all around the planet, touching every continent, most nations. Home to tens of millions of species, everything from the submicroscopic to the immense.

You feel small beside a whale. Insignificant. Then you realize that a whale is insignificant in the ocean.

And then you're flying over the bare fringe of that ocean, flying over a mystery that puny Homo sapiens may never fully understand.

And you feel your own smallness, your own utter weakness, and it's like a lead weight on your chest.

It's not that the ocean is an enemy. It simply doesn't care. It feeds you, it makes the oxygen you breathe, it gave birth to your species, and, if you get careless, it kills you. All without the slightest personal interest.

There's nothing you can say to the ocean. No mercy to be begged. No deals to be made. If we were weak or careless or stupid, it would smother us, crush us, bury us forever in miles of black, black water.

<Rachel?>

<WHAT?> I yelped, shaken out of my dark imaginings.

<I was going to ask how you're doing,> Tobias said. Then, after a moment of silence, he said, <Big, isn't it?>

<Yeah. It's large.>

Too big for all my bravado. And I was going down into its very heart. Like a lunatic, I'd cheated in order to face it first. Now I was dragging poor Tobias right along with me.

And I was supposed to like him.

After more than an hour of flying, Jake landed on the swelling, heaving surface of the sea. We'd followed the rough directions of the Chee.

I landed, too. Easy enough for the seagull brain, which had no particular concerns.

The ocean was frigid, the wet cold held at bay by my fluffed, oily feathers.

A dangerous place for a human. Worse for a hawk.

Tobias landed beside me, bobbing like a white-and-black cork on the swells.

<Okay, we'll demorph and remorph one at a time,> Jake said. <Cassie first. Tobias last.>

Within minutes, Cassie had morphed from seagull to human, then on to sleek, playful dolphin. This made me feel better. Having a helpful dolphin around is like having a couple dozen lifeguards on hand.

<Come on in, Jake,> she called, giddy from the dolphin brain. <The water's fine!> She dived and shot up through the air, then twisted and nosed down for a no-splash dive.

One by one, we did the same. The passage through human morph was not fun. Seagulls ride the waves. Humans end up swallowing saltwater and imagining sharks rising up from the depths.

I don't think Ax enjoyed it any more than we did. He can swim, but it's an awkward thing to see.

Tobias landed on Cassie's back, demorphed to hawk, then waited for me to catch up, riding Cassie's back with his talons dug sharply into her rubbery gray flesh.

<Whale time,> Tobias said to me.

"Yeah," I yelled, treading water and spitting brine. "Let's do it."

<I had a premonition she'd say that,> Marco teased.

Okay, here goes nothing, I thought, as Cassie and Marco swam up alongside me and I summoned a mental picture of the whale.

Saltwater splashed my face. Again and again. I swallowed it. Gagged.

My bones stretched and grew heavy, my

97

feathered arms flapped frantically until fingers sprouted and I could tread water.

I was tired. Eyes burning, I glanced over at Tobias.

His red-tailed hawk form was already shifting. He slipped from Cassie's back into the water.

I closed my eyes and visualized the sperm whale.

And felt the changes begin.

CHAPTER 19

Big. Bigger. Enormous.

I was expanding, stretching in every direction at once.

Huge!

Only I wasn't a whale.

I've mentioned that morphs get weird? That things don't happen in some nice, neat, gradual way? Well, this morph was ridiculous.

I was growing, growing, growing! My skin had turned leathery graphite gray. There was a blow-hole in the back of my neck. My head was monstrous and out of proportion.

But the rest of me was still Rachel. I had a head the size of Iowa. And about an acre of floating blond hair.

<Oh, man!> Marco groaned. <Oh, I didn't need to see this! Rachel, you have pores as big as potholes!>

<This is definitely bizarre,> Cassie said. <And not in a good way.>

I glanced at Tobias. He seemed to be morphing normally. If any morph is ever normal. If a creature with feathers melting into flesh is normal.

<This is ridiculous,> Jake complained. <I am tangled in your hair!>

<She's sinking!> Ax said. <Her buoyancy has not adjusted. She has dense human tissues.>

<I do not,> I said, vaguely offended. But he was right: I was sinking.

And if I didn't finish morphing, I was going to drown. Probably sink to the bottom and float past the Pemalite ship. A big, drowned, female Gulliver.

That got me back on track.

My legs blended. My feet flattened.

My head bulged into a huge rectangle. My eyes slid apart . . . apart till they were in separate zip codes. My neck thickened and a triangular dorsal hump grew out of my back along my spine.

My skin shriveled.

My arms slithered back into my body. Flippers sprouted.

I bobbed to the surface. My blowhole inhaled. My lungs filled.

I felt the water ripple as the dolphins surged and danced.

I sensed their joy and felt a deep, thousand-generation-old kinship with my lithe, sleek brethren.

My instincts were sure. Calm. Confident.

I had no fear. No questions.

I asked for nothing. I explained nothing.

I drew a deep breath, expanding my lungs to their full capacity and dove, arching my dorsal hump and flipping my triangular fluke into the air.

The ocean was no longer a cold and hostile place.

It was home.

I knew its temperatures and depths, its floors and crevices.

I fired off a blast of pulsed clicks and received a "picture" of everything around me. Like a black-and-white sketch that traced across my mind and was erased like an Etch-A-Sketch.

I was echolocating. I had natural sonar.

I "saw" the dolphins and they "saw" me.

And then another large creature was moving toward me.

<Rachel, I sure hope that's you,> Tobias called.

Oh. Right.

The whale brain wasn't hard to control.

The thing was, I hadn't even tried.

I'd liked the calm confidence. The absence of fear.

<It's definitely me,> I said, rolling and powering my gigantic, muscled body up, up, up toward dim light like a runaway train.

Another train rushed beside me. We raced to the barrier between sky and sea.

<Yah-HAH!> Tobias shouted as we exploded the barrier and erupted into the sky. Our massive heads surged into the crisp air, water shimmering down around us.

<Okay, that was cool,> Jake said.

<I wanna be a sperm whale,> Marco whined.

<I don't think so,> Jake said. <Ticktock. We need to stay on track here.>

<Just need to suck some air,> I said.

I exhaled, spouting spray and drawing in enough air to last to maximum dive capacity. Passages in my massive head filled with water and, all automatically, the waxy deposits of spermaceti cooled the water and sent me plunging.

Ten thousand feet. Maybe even twelve thousand feet.

Into giant squid territory. I hoped.

Where the atmospheric pressure could squeeze every last molecule of air from a human body.

<Ready, Rachel?> Tobias asked.

<Ready,> I said, sighing and shivering deep in my soul. The whale might not be scared. I was.

CHAPTER 20

We arched our backs and sounded, slipping silently down into the living sea.

We descended quickly, echolocating past shelves and hollows, our sonar drawing us sketchy, uncertain pictures.

Murky shadows and then, total darkness.

Total. Like being blind. Like having your eyes taped shut and being locked in an underground vault.

Lightless.

The whale's senses quickened. The whale did not hear, but it did anticipate. We'd soon be entering the hunting grounds.

Where my prey sometimes fought me and won.

<Hey, Rachel, did you know that not only do sperm whales eat squid, but some people think squid eat sperm whales?> Tobias said helpfully.

<No one really knows what giant squid eat,> I said. <Except for the fact that they are cannibals.>

<Oh, good. Well, we both did our research.>

<Yeah. I feel so much better now.>

From my memory I called up the brief bit I'd read about squid. They had sharp, parrotlike beaks and eight arms covered with grasping, needle-toothed suckers. And two long, powerful tentacles that worked to grab prey at a distance and draw it toward the arms and mouth.

It occurred to me that I didn't know how whales killed squid.

But I could more than imagine how squid killed whales.

Still, we powered down into the darkness. Falling, falling forever through darkness.

The whale did not fear what was going to happen.

It hunted to eat every day. Someone would win the battle, someone would lose. The whale had accepted this fact since birth.

I had not. Losing was not something I wanted to think about. This was not a situation where I could simply demorph if the whale was hurt.

To demorph was to die.

<So, Rachel, what's new?> Tobias called, sounding, if possible, even jumpier than I felt.

I blurted out the only new thing I could think of. <Well, a guy named T. T. asked me to go to the movies with him.>

WHAT? What made me say *that*?

If I could've kicked myself, I would have.

<T. T., huh? What does that stand for? Troubled Teen? Total Turmoil? Terrible Trauma?> Tobias said sarcastically.

<I don't know and I don't particularly care,> I shot back, irked by his attitude.

<Well, you should care if you're going out with him,> Tobias said.

<Well, if I was, then I would,> I snapped.

<Oh.> Silence. <Why aren't you going out with him?>

<Why do you want to know?> I countered. I could play that game, too.

<I don't, I'm just making conversation,> he said. <We can't exactly turn on the TV and veg out.>

<Well, if you don't want to know, then I'm not going to tell you,> I said, firing off a burst of pulsed clicks and studying the "picture" I got back.

<Rachel —> he began.

But I didn't want to talk about T. T. anymore and I especially didn't want to tell Tobias why I hadn't accepted the date. This was so *not* the time.

<How are we supposed to catch this squid? If we even find one?> I said instead. <I mean, squid are fast and the whale can't exactly turn on a dime here. What do we do, just hang around with our mouths open and hope a squid swims in?>

<I'm not sure,> Tobias admitted. <The thing I read said maybe whales can use echolocation to stun prey. I think that's what it said. Wasn't it?>

<I guess we'll find out. See that shape, that bunch of dots all moving together?>

<See? I don't *see* anything. Oh, you mean on echolocation. Yeah. Like a school of fish.>

<Could be squid. Little ones, not giants. The whale brain wants them. Maybe they're squid.>

<This is no way to hunt,> Tobias complained. <You need to see your prey. I mean, that's basic.>

<For a hawk, anyway,> I said.

<For any sensible predator. This is nuts. Chasing an echolocation picture.>

<I'm going to see if it's true. That we can stun them.>

CLICK-CLICK-CLICK-CLICK-CLICK.

I fired a round of clicks, maximum volume, directing the sound toward the sketchy tornado of squid. Suddenly a part of the swarm stopped moving. <Cool.>

<It doesn't last long,> Tobias commented.

I had noticed that, too. <And these squid are, what, maybe a foot long? We're talking about something that can stretch out and grab both baskets on a basketball court. Let's see how stunned the big boy is. If we ever find him.>

<Hey, Rachel,> Tobias said. <How long you figure we've been down?>

<Twenty minutes? Four hours? Who can tell?> I said gloomily. <I'm starting to feel the pressure. My whale's brain is getting edgy.>

The whale part of me wanted to surface. The human part of me had wanted to do that for a long time.

<Let's split up,> I said. <Maybe spread out.>

<Or maybe surface and come back down again.>

<I don't want to have to do this again,> I said. <This gives me the major creeps.>

<You got that right. I'll veer off. We need a big squid and a bigger spaceship.>

We searched, echolocating for what felt like forever. Back and forth and always, always down. Once I picked up something that might have been a giant squid. But I lost him.

It was madness! We were blundering around blindly. The sun's rays had never reached this depth. Never. If the water had been rock and dirt, it could not have been any darker.

We were buried alive!

Buried alive in water.

<Gotta surface,> Tobias said at last, his thought-speak voice faint, his tone shaken.

<Yeah,> I agreed.

We turned and headed up. And now the panic grew. You can walk through a graveyard at night and be afraid, but the terror doesn't begin to get you till you start to run away. When you acknowledge fear, it grows. And although I tried to tell myself it wasn't terror sending me to the surface, that it was just a need for air, I knew better.

We raced. We barreled madly toward the surface. It took forever. Up and up and up.

Air! Where was the air?

We'd been down too long. We'd never reach the sky again. We were going to die in darkness, to sink and sink back to the cold, lightless, lifeless ocean floor.

Buried alive in water.

CHAPTER 21

I kicked hard, every muscle in my massive body straining, desperate now. Desperate!

Then . . .

FWOOOOOSH!

I exploded into the air, exploded out of the water, blew the stale air from my lungs, and crashed back into the sea.

Ka-WHUMP!

Tobias erupted a quarter mile away.

I sucked air. I exhaled and inhaled and sucked air like I was never going to breathe again.

The others in dolphin morph were nowhere around. I was actually surprised, though I should have known better. You can't travel miles down through water and come popping back up in a straight line.

Tobias wallowed in the waves beside me.

<We could morph to something with wings,> he suggested. <Find the others.>

<And tell them what?> I demanded, angry at myself now. <Tell them we gave up?>

<You want to go back down there?> he asked like I was crazy.

<I don't know,> I admitted.

<Oh, man. So we find the others, tell them we failed? Then what?>

I knew then what. So did Tobias. Jake would take us all back to the beach. This time he'd acquire and morph the whale, along with Cassie or Marco.

So one of them would be back here. With even less time. With even less chance of success.

<This is so not fun,> Tobias said.

<Yeah. I know. Sorry I got you into this.>

<Oh, shut up,> he said tolerantly. <Let's go.>

Down again. Down and down and down. Into the water like ink.

Ten minutes down we split up again. <Don't go too far,> Tobias called after me.

I probably should have listened to him.

I swam hard. I fired off round after round of pulsed clicks. Picture after picture came back to me. Revealing nothing big enough to be the ship or the squid.

And then, suddenly . . .

A flash of light! A shimmering, rippling light!

I almost laughed. Fish! Phosphorescent fish, their pale, chemical-reaction glow like a neon sign in the blackness.

The fish were moving away from me, but at an angle. Like they were moving away from something else. From something behind me, to my left and —

I fired clicks. The picture came back with startling clarity. The details were unmistakable.

Coming toward me through the water like a dark, deadly torpedo was a hungry, angry, sixty-foot giant squid.

So much for the question of whether squid are aggressive, I thought. Someday the six of us could write a serious update of zoology textbooks. If we lived that long.

<Tobias!> I shouted. I fired off a frenzy of machine-gunned clicks at the squid.

It staggered, stumbled in its charge.

<Tobias!> I yelled again, as the whale's instincts took over. It wanted to kill the squid. It wanted to hunt.

Where was Tobias?

Hunt, yes. Kill, no. We needed the squid alive. The whale didn't care. This was core instinct. This was hunger and the urge to hunt. I fought the whale's brain. It had been so docile I'd almost not noticed it. But that was only because I'd done what the whale wanted me to do.

Now I could feel the power of that huge, intelligent brain as it fought to carry out the instructions encoded deep in its DNA.

And while I was doing that, the squid recovered and came at me with murder in its blood.

From far away, a faint voice. Tobias!

<I think I found the Pemalite ship,> Tobias called faintly.

<Great. I found the squid.>

CHAPTER 22

A whip in the darkness. I never saw it coming. It slapped against me, gripping, hugging, holding.

Another!

The two almost thirty-foot-long tentacles, iron-strong arms, tightened around my head.

The squid used the tentacles to yank the rest of its body toward me. I felt the tug. I felt the water moving. I could picture the photograph I'd seen of a squid mouth, a bizarre hawk's beak.

Then an arm, thicker, stronger than the tentacle. And another!

I thrashed wildly, tearing free one of the arms. The suckers ripped away chunks of my skin. I smelled my own blood in the water.

My tail! I couldn't move it. And the squid was on me. ON me! Too close for echolocation to see anything. I was wrestling blind. And unlike the squid, I had no arms.

The squid was smaller, much lighter, basically weaker. But it had agility. And it had arms. I had a mouth.

Imagine a fight between a gymnast, small but with full use of arms and legs, and a three-hundred-pound linebacker who can only use his mouth.

The squid was locking me up. And now I was sinking.

Down to where the atmospheric pressure would crush even me.

Down to where my burning lungs would force me to exhale.

Down to black death.

<NO!>

I lunged and rolled. The squid hung on. I hammered it with pulsed clicks. Again and again! But my own body mass was helping to shield it.

I echolocated again and again, but it was on me. Then, one burst of clicks caught a wall of denser water and bounced back. It drew me a fragmented, eerie picture.

The squid was huge! Its arrow-shaped head, long as a small school bus, was pressed close to my head. Its sharp, snapping beak was only inches from my left eye. Eight twenty-foot arms and two longer tentacles clutched and tore at me. Sharp-edged suckers the size of saucers Super Glued the creature to me.

I was weakening.

It couldn't be!

No, I begged. *No, it couldn't happen!*

But the squid's grip tightened, tightened, relentless, like a python, imprisoning my tail, paralyzing me.

CLICK-CLICK-CLICK-CLICK-CLICK!

Whale clicks. But not from me!

<Tobias!>

<Hang on, Rachel, I'm here!> Tobias cried and fired again.

The squid convulsed. I felt its spasm of pain. Its arms fell away from me.

<Tobias . . . the fight . . . used too much air . . . I have to get to the surface!>

<Go,> he said tersely. <I'll meet you there.>

I wanted to stay. I should have stayed.

If the squid killed Tobias . . .

No choice!

<Go!> Tobias yelled. He blasted the squid with another round of clicks, up close and personal.

I went. I had no choice. The whale's brain was screaming.

I rose fast, but still it was forever and forever.

The whale was weakening. Faltering. Its senses were cloudy, unsure. Confused.

<Rachel? Tobias? Is that one of you coming up? We've been searching . . .>

Cassie's voice. Close, so close.

<Me,> I said dully. <Whale's had it. Too tired.>

<No! Make it swim! You're only a few yards from the surface! Do it!> Cassie yelled.

Swim, I told myself, forcing my aching body to move. *Swim!*

This time I didn't explode into the air. I rose, half-unconscious, too exhausted even to appreciate the air that was filling my lungs.

<Where's Tobias?> Cassie asked, bobbing up beside me.

<The squid. Down fighting the squid,> I said exhaustedly. <I have to go back. Have to help him.>

<No,> Cassie said. <No.>

Another dolphin shot up alongside me.

<Rachel?> Jake said.

<I have to help Tobias!>

<Thanks, but no help necessary,> Tobias said.

<Tobias!>

<Of course. Just me and my squid. Hah! Hawk or whale, there is no prey I can't take down. Coming up. Look out above.>

117

<Everyone careful,> I yelled as the others arrived on the scene. <Don't let it grab you!>

<Wow,> Marco said, as the squid's scarlet mantle came into view. <Talk about a face only a mother could love!>

<It probably ate its mother,> I said grimly, moving in for the kill. <And now I'm gonna eat it.>

<Uh, I don't think so, Rachel,> Tobias said. <I didn't go to all this trouble just for you to kill it. Just cripple it.>

<I've got it,> I said, lunging.

Now, by the light of the stars and moon, I could see the squid's huge, black eyes the size of hubcaps, the largest eyes on Earth, looking straight into mine.

It slapped me with a grasping whip tentacle.

I bit it off.

Thick, green blood gushed from the stump.

I clamped my powerful mouth down on several squid arms and held on. Tobias did the same.

Two against one. We had the squid outnumbered.

CHAPTER 23

I kept the now-helpless squid on the surface as Jake, Cassie, Marco, Ax, and finally Tobias acquired it. It wasn't easy. It wasn't exactly a party, as human and Andalite and hawk wallowed in the waves, pressing hands and talons against the rubbery creature.

Fortunately the squid responded normally to being acquired. It grew calm and peaceful.

<Your turn, Rachel,> Jake said.

I demorphed, shrinking from building size to human size. The demorph was a bit more normal than the morph. I shrank in proportion for most of it.

Then, at last, I was just a very out-of-place

girl, up to my neck in cold saltwater stained with squid ink and blood. I treaded water to stay near the cephalopod's big arrow head. I needed to touch the creature. I ended up swallowing about a gallon of inky seawater. I had to extend the acquiring phase to hold the squid still for Tobias.

Like I said. Not exactly a party.

When we were done I morphed back to whale to haul the squid away to a safe distance. Once released the poor squid took off, jetting down into the relative safety of the water beneath us.

"Well, this should be bleah" — Marco spit saltwater out of his mouth — "should be interesting."

<I think this will be an interesting morph,> Ax said. <So many arms.>

"Let's just get it over with," I said, having resumed my human form. "It's a long, long way down. And we don't have a lot of time."

<Two of your hours and seven of your minutes,> Ax said.

"Ax, they are everyone's hours and everyone's minutes," Marco said. "My hours are your hours. This is Earth. A minute is a minute!"

<Now we have two of your hours and six of your minutes,> Ax said dryly.

"Tobias? Can you get us back to where you found the ship?" Jake asked.

Tobias was being held more or less up out of the water by Jake and Cassie. He was not a happy bird.

<I can try,> he said.

"Okay. Everyone morph. Let's get this done."

I have experienced many unusual morphs. I have been more different animals than most people ever see. I thought I was ready for anything.

But this was weird.

I focused my mind and felt the changes begin.

You don't actually "feel" the things that happen during a morph. You sort of feel them from a distance. The way you might feel the dentist's drill, even through the Novocain.

It's not exactly pain. But not exactly normal, either.

I could hear a squishing sound coming from inside me, from my guts. And then I reached down and felt my stomach sinking inward.

My internal organs were slithering away to hang in Zero-space until I returned to claim them. I was being scooped out!

My arms and legs began to stretch. Out and out, farther and farther, absurdly, idiotically far. My arms formed the clubbed ends that marked them as tentacles. My legs were two of the eight normal arms.

Normal. Right.

Sploot! Sploot!

More arms were poking out of me, writhing out of my chest and back and sides, six new arms, like snakes crawling out through my flesh and growing as they emerged.

I had the horrific image of being an egg, hatching snakes. I was all writhing arms.

<Well, there's a whole new nightmare,> I muttered.

And now, all down the bizarrely extended arms, hundreds of saucer-sized, needle-toothed bumps, popped up like sores.

Flimp!

My head imploded. Just suddenly sagged, as my skull melted away. My eyes spread wide and the top of my head started growing out and out, like some cartoon of an out-of-control zit. And my insides seemed to percolate up into that head area.

My skin turned brown. It hung from me like a sweatshirt ten sizes too big. It was like wearing a cape. A cape of powerful muscle.

My eyes became huge, circular pools of darkness. I had sunk down into the water, maybe fifty, eighty feet, not counting my arms, which extended farther still. But I could still see. The squid's eyes were as good as an owl's at seeing in low light. Maybe better.

Then, as I slowly tested my arms, as the hundreds of suction cups tensed and released, I felt the squid mind rise up beneath my own.

Other squid! All around me.

And I was hungry.

So hungry.

CHAPTER 24

Someone was turned away from me. Another giant squid, floating, arms extended like some vile flower. I saw the mantle.

My meat.

I drew in water and expelled it like a jet blowing exhaust.

I jetted forward! I drew my long arms up from the depths, coiling them and extending them toward my prey, moving them in what felt to the human part of me like slow motion.

The other squid was unaware!

Cassie? Was it Cassie?

Who cared? Cassie would feed my hunger just as well as —

She jerked at my touch. Her own arms whipped back toward me.

<Hey!> she protested.

<Oh . . . oh, sorry,> I said. The human me had regained the upper hand. <I was just . . . >

<I know what you "were just,"> Cassie sniffed. <I had the same problem. But I didn't start to eat *you*.>

<I said I'm sorry.>

<All right,> Jake said. <Tobias? Lead the way.>

Easy to say. Almost impossible to do. People think diving is like taking an elevator down. But we were talking about three miles of water. Three *miles* of currents and crosscurrents. In darkness so total that after the first mile or so even the squid's specially adapted eye could see nothing. Not to mention the fact that there was nothing to see!

There were two clocks ticking in our heads: a little over two hours till the nuclear vault opened and a paralyzed Chee was discovered.

And just two hours till we were trapped in morph.

And one major complication: If we demorphed, we'd be crushed, our bodies squeezed flat till the bones would stick out of us like pins in a pin-

cushion, our heads popped like overripe can-
taloupes.

Which meant there was a third clock: the
point of no return. The point beyond which we'd
no longer have time to get back to the surface.
Beyond that point we either found the Pemalite
ship or . . .

But Tobias was not finding the ship. The ship
was huge. Maybe three hundred feet long, ac-
cording to the Chee. But imagine that you know
where a three-hundred-foot-long building is.
Then you leave the building and walk three miles
through darkness.

Now imagine finding your way back. Blind-
folded.

We reached the ocean floor and Tobias led us
this way and that. Back and forth, skimming like
mushy torpedoes across dead desert wastes, our
jets kicking up clouds of sand and tiny rocks and
the decayed remains of everything that had ever
died in the three miles of water above us.

Now and then, a flash of phosphorescence.
And then, darkness again.

<I screwed up,> Tobias said. <I should have
stayed in whale morph! I can't echolocate! I'm
going on instinct here. This is insane!>

<We are now at the point of no return,> Ax re-
ported. <We turn back . . . or hope to find the
Pemalite ship.>

<We have to bail, Jake,> Tobias said, sounding defeated. <This isn't working.>

<This mission has bombed from the start!> Marco said, exploding in the same frustration we all felt. <Getting jerked around by someone, we don't even know who or what. It's all a setup and I'm —>

<Wait!> Cassie said. <I see lights!>

<Just those glowing fish,> I said.

<No. No. Look!>

It was impossible to tell distance in the blank, black sea, but yes, there were lights! A string of them, descending in a downhill line.

<Seven . . . eight . . . I count eight,> Jake said.

<What are they?> I wondered.

Marco made a snorting sound in our heads. <Can't you guess? Yeerks.>

CHAPTER 25

<I do not think the odds favor us,> Ax said with cool understatement.

<This time you're wrong, Ax-man,> Tobias said. <They're going the same place we are. Following the signal from the ship.>

<Pointing the way!> Cassie said.

<Haul butt!> Jake said.

We hauled. Suck in water . . . blow it out . . . draw it in . . . blow it out . . .

We jetted along the ocean floor, heading for the place where the string of lights pointed. Were we closer? Were they? Impossible to say.

Then . . .

<Whoa!> I felt, rather than saw, the ground open beneath me, a vast deep canyon. And

there, perched comfortably on a shelf just below the canyon lip, glowing faintly green, was what could only be a ship.

Not a human ship.

It was, as the Chee had said, about three hundred feet long. They had not told us what it looked like. But the faint green outline was strikingly clear: The Pemalite ship was shaped like a sort of clownish version of one of them. Like someone had done a cartoon of a Pemalite, exaggerating the vaguely canine head, making the slender hind legs stubby, the belly chubby.

<It looks like Snoopy!> Cassie said.

It did. Kind of. Like a huge, prone, faint green Snoopy.

<Not exactly the Blade ship, is it?> Jake said.

<The Pemalites didn't build it to be a weapon,> Cassie said. <It's a toy. They built it for fun.>

I looked up. The line of Yeerk ships was still above us. Maybe a mile. Maybe a hundred feet. <Let's get inside.>

We jetted over. The outer hull access panel was clearly, conveniently lit.

<Here's the environmental adaptation panel Erek told us about,> Jake said, placing a row of suckers on top of the flat rectangle. <Let's see what the Pemalite computer makes of this.>

A glowing yellow light flashed twice, to our eyes as blindingly bright as a flashbulb.

Jake drew back his long squid arm, and using just the tip, daintily punched the number six.

Immediately, the side of the ship slid open, exposing a decompression chamber big enough to accommodate six giant squid.

<Cool,> Marco said, following us inside. <It might as well just say, "Hello, giant squid. Party of six?">

I glanced back as the decompression door began to close on a stew of giant tentacles and arms. The lights outside were larger now. Closer.

The entire ship began to brighten, like a lightbulb on a dimmer switch.

It illuminated the rock shelf. It illuminated a pair of hideous fish. And it illuminated the closest of what looked very much like eight Bug fighters.

The outer door shut.

<We have company coming,> I said.

<Let's get this done. We have to get in and turn off the signal,> Jake said.

An inner door began to open.

<Erek said we'd have an atmosphere designed to sustain our life-forms,> Jake said. <Hope they're prepared for squid.>

<Yeah. Ready with batter and hot boiling oil. Calamari for ten thousand,> Marco said.

We were gently extruded through the door into the ship. The interior lights came up, slowly. And Erek was right. There was an environment waiting for us.

<Oh. My. God.> Cassie said.

We were still swimming. Still in water. Sort of.

We were each suspended above the floor in a personal, floating bubble of water. Like a water blimp.

I jetted. The bubble moved. I reached a hand through the water bubble into the air beyond. I felt dryness. The bubble did not collapse.

<Oh, man, if we could take this technology, we could open a water park that would totally rule the world of water parks,> Marco said.

<Yeah, that was my first thought, too,> I said. <Water park dominance.>

Beyond the bubble was a world of magic.

Lush green-and-purple grass carpeted the floor, forming patterns: swirls, checkerboards, Picasso-like abstracts and Van Gogh flowers. Trees and bushes in Crayola colors grew in thickets and hushed groves. A sparkling river meandered through the center of the ship, cascading down into a gentle waterfall and a rippling lake below.

Everywhere there were inexplicable, brightly colored, gaily lit machines that could only be toys of some sort. Beside us, wafting through the air, were things like long, feathered snakes. Projected on the arched ceiling, far overhead, were patterns of clouds and skies like nothing on Earth.

After all the thousands of years, it was all still working. Only the dead silence lay as a grim reminder of a species lost.

<Where is the bridge?> Ax demanded.

<Kind of like your Dome ship, Ax-man, only much cooler,> Tobias said.

<Yes, well, we had to make room for weapons,> Ax said disparagingly. <Which is why Andalites still exist and Pemalites do not.>

<Touchy, touchy,> Marco said.

<There must be a bridge,> Ax said. <Even these space-going children had to have a bridge.>

<That tree?> Cassie suggested <I see lights and stuff.>

We jetted, contained within our water balloons, and came to the tree. Sure enough, a series of fairly businesslike panels were fitted into the trunk.

<This is absurd,> Ax said. <The bridge is a tree trunk? We Andalites love trees, but this is ludicrous.>

<Turn off the signal, and let's get out of here before the Yeerks get in,> Jake said.

On one panel a red light blinked. Below it was a button.

<I'm thinking push that button,> Marco offered.

Ax's water bubble slowly pushed aside Marco's. <Perhaps I had better take care of this,> Ax said.

A cheerful thought-speak voice sang out in our heads. <Greetings, friends. We are happy to have you aboard. However, we would not want you to access this panel. It is possible that you might accidentally do yourself harm. And that would be so sad.>

Ax punched in the number six.

<That is the correct code! Our concerns were misplaced.>

<Now that we've penetrated their crack security . . .> Marco said with a laugh.

<Many thanks, friend. You now have access to the control panel. Make your selection at your convenience. When you are finished, we hope you will join us in a game, a delightful meal, or simply relax and enjoy yourself.>

<This is weird,> I said. <You know, I heard Disney was building a cruise ship. Maybe this is it.>

Ax began communing with the control panel. It didn't take long.

<All normal Chee functions are restored,> the Pemalite voice said. <Would you like something to eat?>

133

And then . . . <Chee destruct sequence has been activated. Are you sure this is what you want? All Chee within range will self-destruct in fifteen minutes.>

<WHAT?> Cassie yelped.

<What happened?> Tobias demanded.

<I don't know,> Ax admitted.

And then, quite suddenly, the black ocean was all around us.

<Ahhh! What the . . .>

<The hull has become transparent,> Ax said, the first to figure it out.

The parklike world was all still there. But the projected sky was gone, replaced by ink water. The outer hull was now like glass. And through that glass I saw the line of Bug fighters. Eight. Lined up outside the decompression chamber.

We could see them.

They could see us.

Through transparent bulkheads, through the transparent hull, through the front viewport of the lead Bug fighter, I saw a hard, cold-eyed Andalite face.

An Andalite face. But the light of malice that shone through the two large eyes, through the twin stalk eyes, was not Andalite.

<Visser Three,> I whispered.

CHAPTER 26

< They don't have the code,> Cassie said.

<The code is a single digit!> Marco said. <How long do you think . . .>

The Bug fighter turned, bringing a modified rear door into contact with the invisible outer hull. A Hork-Bajir bounded inside. A Taxxon slithered behind him. And then, moving almost daintily as he stepped from the Bug fighter down into the Pemalite ship, came Visser Three.

<We can't even morph,> I yelled in frustration. <He can see us!>

The Yeerks broke the code. The outer door of the decompression chamber opened.

The fighters disgorged Hork-Bajir and Taxxons into the Pemalite ship. They formed up around

Visser Three in the decompression chamber, some fanning out to take up flanking positions.

<They'll cut us to ribbons!> Tobias said.

"Oh, dilemma! Oh, drama! Oh, the tension and excitement of it all!"

The voice was new. Not thought-speak. High, shrill, grating.

<Who the . . . what?> Jake said. <Where did that voice come from?>

"Right here, Jake. From me, Big Jake. Jake, the reluctant leader. Jake, the oh-so-tiresomely decent one. A sanctimonious killer: my least favorite kind."

<The puppetmaster,> I said. <The guy behind all this.>

<Where are you?> Jake demanded. <Come out and show yourself.>

"Come out, come out wherever you are," the voice sang mockingly. "Of course. I'll even come out with my hands up."

It appeared from behind a tree. It moved on two legs, body held forward and balanced by a stubby tail. It walked like a bird or a small dinosaur. It did hold its hands up. But they were weak, flimsy things, multiply jointed but obviously designed for very light work or very low gravity.

The head was surprising for that almost reptilian body: vaguely human in shape, with a narrow lower jaw and wide-set, intelligent, laughing eyes.

It was wrinkled, like your thumb after a long bath. Its flesh was dark, almost black. The eyes and mouth were rimmed in green.

<All right. What is that?> Tobias asked Ax.

<That is not a species I recognize.>

<I don't know what species it is, but I think we'd better report it to the Prune Growers Association,> Marco said.

"Oh, Marco the funny one!" the creature cried, slapping its limp hands together. "How's Mommy, Marco? Is she alive or is she dead? Does she scream with the Yeerk in her head?"

Marco reached for the creature with two long tentacles. But neither touched the withered thing. They stopped and bent back.

"All here together?" the prune thing mocked. "Cassie, the hypocrite? 'I don't believe in violence . . . except when I do.' Aximili, the pitiful, pale shadow of his dead brother? If only you'd insisted on going with Elfangor, maybe he'd have lived. Too bad. And Tobias, ah, yes, Tobias. The boy not really so trapped as a bird, eh, but too gutless to resume life as a human? And Rachel. My very favorite Animorph."

The thing smiled a lipless smile. "Rachel, Rachel. Do you feel the adrenaline rush of murderous desire? Do you feel the urge to reach out

137

and destroy me? Of course you do. You and I have that in common."

<Who are you?> I snapped, trying to ignore the rage it had so clearly seen inside me. Trying to ignore the fear, as well. This thing knew us. All about us. Who we were, what we were. All it had to do was to tell the Yeerks. Then, even if we escaped, we were finished.

"Haven't figured it out yet? Ooh, so slow. Allow me to introduce myself," it said. "I am the Drode. It's a word from my species. It means 'wild card.'"

<Crayak,> Jake said. <You're *his* creature.>

"Oh, very clever, Big Jake, Prince Jake. Have you killed your brother yet? No? Well, you will."

<Crayak sent you,> Jake answered calmly. <Payback?>

The Drode grinned. Then the grin disappeared. "Payback," it said. "You ruined his Howlers. Ruined his plan for the Iskoort. Crayak doesn't like you, Big Jake. Any of you." Then it looked straight at me. "Although *you* have potential."

I let that go by. I didn't want to think about what it meant. <This is all your setup,> I said. <Causing the Chee malfunction. Setting things up so we could escape from the mall unnoticed. Killing that sperm whale. And now, starting a self-destruct for the Chee.>

138

"Whale killing? Me?" the Drode said in mock horror. "No, no, no. That big lump on the beach falls just over the line into sentience. And I never kill a sentient creature. Your whale will survive."

<The rules,> Ax said. <You still must live within the rules that govern the Ellimist and Crayak.>

"Yes, yes, oh yes," the Drode sneered. "Mustn't upset the balance. Not directly, anyway. But! Create problems? Yes. Create opportunities? Yes. Play the wild card? Of course. And now, no more time for chat. The Yeerks are here for you. Will they kill you outright? Or will they make you Controllers? I don't care. Either way, my master will reward me."

<I thought you couldn't kill sentient creatures,> Cassie said desperately. <That's the rule, isn't it? But you set the self-destruct for the Chee.>

The Drode laughed. "They're machines, you silly girl. Androids."

<You're killing us,> Tobias said. <Putting us in an impossible situation. We can't morph here in plain view of the Yeerks. You know that. You know we can't fight back. That's the same as killing us. Murder.>

"Nonsense," the Drode said. "There's always a way left for you. That's also part of the rules. Now, if you don't find it, well . . ."

The creature walked back behind a tree. A tree much too narrow to conceal it. And yet it disappeared.

I looked left. Hork-Bajir and Taxxons were filling the decompression chamber. Twenty, maybe more Hork-Bajir. Half a dozen Taxxons. And Visser Three: an army all by himself.

Trapped!

Demorph, and give up our greatest secret, a secret that protected our families as well as ourselves.

Or simply wait to die.

CHAPTER 27

<It won't take them long to get here. They'll be here in a —> I started to say.

<Ink!> Cassie yelled. <Ink! That's the way out. Shoot your ink. It'll cloud these water bubbles. We'll be out of sight and we can morph without the Yeerks seeing us in human phase!>

<Do it!> Jake yelled. <Ax!>

<Yes, Prince Jake, I know,> he said. Ax only had to demorph. He would have to buy us time.

<Me, too,> Tobias said.

Immediately, a dark, roiling cloud of ink billowed out of me like a dense wall of fog, creeping out farther and farther, blocking and isolating everything in its path.

I couldn't see through it. But I didn't know how long it would last.

I began to demorph. Speed was everything. Ax and Tobias would try to slow the advancing Yeerks. But they wouldn't last more than a few seconds against that army.

I began to shrink, becoming small within the vast bubble. My tentacles rolled up, suckers disappeared, my beak mouth became teeth. Too slow! Soon I'd be a human, sucking on water.

No. Wait! Water. Yeah, it was water. Black water. *Opaque* water.

<Hey! Swim to the top of your bubbles. You can stick your head out to breathe without being seen!> I managed to yell just as my thought-speak cut out.

I was a creature half-cephalopod, half-human, a horror, a hideous slimy thing with blond hair and shriveling tentacles.

I swam straight up. Up through water as inky black as the water outside the ship. My head, my increasingly human head, poked out through the top. Around me was a gently rolling bubble of ink-filled water. I could see the ceiling above, and Tobias flapping hard for altitude. I could see the rounded, down-sloping edges of the flying bubble itself. But I could not see the Yeerks.

And if I couldn't see them, they couldn't see me.

I began to morph again.

Sharp, curved claws as long as paring knives sprouted from my fingertips. Thick, shaggy fur raced across my growing body. Gleaming fangs erupted where my human teeth had been.

I dove down, as any good grizzly could, down through the black bubble. I swam straight down. Down till my huge, shaggy head erupted from the bottom of the bubble. The bottom of the bubble was about ten feet off the grassy floor.

Suddenly, I dropped.

WHAM!

I landed on my shoulder. I rolled and bounded up to my feet.

The others were dropping around me. A tiger slipped from the bubble nearest mine and landed with all the easy grace my bear lacked. A wolf. A gorilla.

The huge black bubbles continued to float over our heads like very low storm clouds. Ahead of us, a hundred feet away, no more, stood Ax.

Facing Ax, a small Yeerk army.

Lying on the ground were two Taxxons, huge, needle-legged centipedes. They'd been sliced open by an Andalite tail blade. The other Taxxons devoured them noisily, round red mouths descending to rip and tear their brothers.

Visser Three himself had a gash that had almost removed one of his stalk eyes.

Tobias's handiwork.

But the lull was temporary. The Visser was getting ready to renew the attack.

<I don't like these odds,> Marco said.

<I like them better now than five minutes ago,> I said.

<So,> Visser Three said. <We meet again. For the last time. You will never leave this ship alive. And this one . . .> He jerked his hand toward a Hork-Bajir. In the Hork-Bajir's clawed hands, a hawk. <This one dies first!>

I didn't hesitate, I didn't think. I dropped to all fours and charged.

Sheer, massive aggression.

But then, a movement! A Taxxon motoring across my path!

I slammed into it like a tractor rolling over a snail.

"SKKKRREEEEE!" it shrieked. I flailed back in shock and pain. I sank my teeth into its head. Its foul taste flooded my mouth. I whipped my head in fury, tearing the Taxxon in two.

I raked its still-squirming upper body with my claws, shoving it aside. But my charge had been ruined. My chance lost.

With a loud roar — animal, Hork-Bajir, and Taxxon — the battle erupted. We charged; they charged. We exploded into each other.

<Behind you, Rachel!> Ax yelled.

I caught a blurred movement.

Turned as the Hork-Bajir's sharp, razor-bladed arm fell like an ax and buried itself in my hip.

Agony exploded in my brain, driving me into frenzy.

"RRROOOAAARRR!" I screamed, twisting away, staggering as the pain shot a thousand burning spikes through my body.

Cassie leaped and buried her teeth in the back of a Hork-Bajir's neck.

I closed my jaws around the Hork-Bajir. I shook him until he flopped like a rag doll.

I tossed him away.

The battle raged, the lush, peaceful, Pemalite ship a nightmare scene of screams and roars, blood and rage.

"Guhroooar!" Marco, in gorilla morph, leaped down from an outcropping of rocks and tore into a Taxxon.

"SSSRRREEEE-wah!" It fell, writhing, squirming, its lobster-clawed hands clicking and snapping in its death throes.

A sleek, powerful tiger hurtled by, pouncing on a Hork-Bajir's back and burying its fangs in his neck.

The Hork-Bajir staggered. Screamed. Collapsed.

Three huge, fearsome Hork-Bajir had converged on Ax and backed him to the edge of the small lake.

One darted forward, swiping at Ax with his bladed arm.

Lightning-quick, Ax's wicked, scorpion tail flashed.

The severed arm flew and plopped into the lake.

The Hork-Bajir moaned and fell.

The other two advanced.

Growling, I thundered toward them.

Rose up on my back legs.

And stumbled, pitching sideways as my wounded leg gave out, sending me crashing into a Hork-Bajir and knocking him to the ground beneath me.

For one, brief moment our eyes met.

And suddenly, eerily, we were more than warriors on separate sides.

We were each other.

And for a frozen moment, the world went still. Then . . .

Slash!

His arm came up, wrist blade out. I jerked my head back and rolled into him. He slashed again and caught me in the side. I twisted and brought my right paw around. I didn't have the leverage to slash. Instead, I did what a grizzly wouldn't: I drew back my fist and punched him in the face.

I clambered up off his unconscious body.

The battle was everywhere. And we were losing. The grass was littered with fallen Taxxons and Hork-Bajir. The air was thick with dying screams and clogged with the hot, coppery stench of blood.

"*Ghafrash*!" A Hork-Bajir, charging Jake.

Jake slashing, roaring.

Cassie, hobbling, dragging a broken back leg, snarling and dodging a Taxxon's claws.

Marco, bleeding, cheek laid open, his huge, powerful hands wrapped tightly around a Hork-Bajir's neck. Squeezing.

Ax, whirling, slicing, the master of deadly perfection.

But we were losing. Because all alone, surrounded by his Hork-Bajir guard, Visser Three was morphing. Growing. Some hideous creation from some far-distant planet.

Huge! Deadly.

We couldn't defeat all his Hork-Bajir and Taxxons. Let alone this monster.

"Ah-hah-hah! Wonderful! Lovely! Perfect!" the Drode cackled happily. "I love the smell of battle. Oh, J-a-a-ake? Are you dead yet?"

It had reappeared, stepping out from behind the same tree, seemingly oblivious to any danger.

<You. At least I'll take you down,> I said.

The Drode grinned its green-rimmed grin.

"You know, Crayak could use you, Rachel. Why stay with these weaklings? You're already more like us than like them."

<A job offer? How nice.>

"Yes, isn't it? You can survive this debacle. Just do us one small favor: Kill your tiresome cousin. Crayak would like to see that. So would I. Kill Jake."

I laughed. <Kill Jake? Nah. I think I'd rather kill you.>

I lunged for the Drode.

It dodged me easily.

My momentum carried me past it, straight into a pair of Hork-Bajir.

Slash!

My other rear leg buckled. Buckled like it was made out of rubber.

I rose halfway up on all fours, but I couldn't reach the Hork-Bajir. They laughed, seeing I was done for. Laughed at me, at my helplessness.

Then . . . something new. Something steel and ivory, moving at a speed no human, no Hork-Bajir, no Andalite could match.

It raced for the tree. Visser Three slapped at it with one of his morphing claws, but the steel-and-ivory creature simply blocked the blow.

<Erek?> I blurted in disbelief, even as a Hork-Bajir leaned over to cut my throat open.

"No! Nooooo!" the Drode groaned in disbelief.

Erek reached the tree. He punched something into the control panel.

The Hork-Bajir was suddenly moving very . . . very . . . slowly. . . .

"Oh, this is not at all what I had in mind," the Drode said.

I rolled aside and reached to gut it.

But my paw was likewise moving very . . . very . . . slowly.

The thought-speak voice of the ship spoke. <Chee self-destruct disabled. And we are very sorry to say that the hostility containment program has been activated. What a shame to spoil our lovely time with fighting. Once repairs have been made on all injured parties, we will have to ask you to leave the ship.>

"And you wonder why Crayak destroyed the Pemalites," the Drode said, enraged. "What tedious creatures they were. Pacifist androids! What is the *point* of machines that cannot kill? They could have ruled the galaxy with their Chee as warriors!"

The battlefield was frozen. Only Erek and the Drode were able to move. Erek calmly lifted Tobias from the Hork-Bajir's grasp.

The Drode came over to me. It took in the violent tableau: me and the two Hork-Bajir.

The Drode leaned close, close enough to whisper so that only I could hear. "Your friends are all relieved. Are you? Are you happy that peace has been restored? Or don't you itch for the chance to press those deadly claws anot' er six inches forward, to tear open that exposed throat?"

The Drode smiled. Cruel. Smirking.

"If you ever find yourself desperate, Rachel. At an end. In need. Remember this: Your cousin's life is your passport to salvation in the arms of Crayak."

Then it was gone.

CHAPTER 28

The Pemalite ship carefully, politely, regretfully, packed the Yeerks, including a furiously enraged Visser Three, back into their modified Bug fighters.

<I'll kill you all! I'll take this ship apart, piece by piece! I'll be back and nothing will stop me! You'll die, all of you, Andalite and . . . and whoever runs this ship, I'll kill you all!> Visser Three said. Repeatedly.

<We are so sorry you had a bad time,> the ship said. <Perhaps we can meet again someday and enjoy some pleasant activities together.>

Once the Yeerks were gone, we morphed and left the way we'd come in. The ship was polite to us, too. But it wanted us gone, just the same.

It had been only ten minutes from the time we turned off the interference with the Chee till the point when Erek arrived at the ship to interrupt the battle. Ten minutes to get from land to a spot three miles underwater. If it had taken fifteen . . .

The Drode was right about one thing: The Chee had powers that would have made the Pemalites masters of the galaxy.

All that power. And all the Pemalites had ever wanted was to play, to learn, to be happy.

Before we reached the surface of the ocean, the Pemalite ship had been moved. This time to a depth only an android could reach.

It was late when we got home. We were tired. Worn and brittle from a day harsh with fighting.

We each told our separate lies to our various parents, and were each grounded. I don't think anyone minded.

I wondered if I should tell Jake about the Drode's foul offer. But I decided against it. I knew I would never, ever give in. I knew myself.

I did. I knew my limits. I knew.

But what the Drode and his evil master Crayak had seen inside of me was real. Jake knew it. He trusted me, but there might come a time when he would doubt . . .

Jake had enough to worry about.

I went running down along the beach the next day. You couldn't even see where the big sperm whale had lain, gasping for breath.

The news had said it was a freak shift in wind, bringing a small tidal surge that had lifted the whale free. Of course, I knew better.

I felt a small shadow pass over me, blocking the sun for just a moment. I didn't even look up. I kept running. Maybe I could find a hidden spot somewhere up ahead and morph.

A few minutes later, "Hey! Rachel?"

I turned, surprised to find T. T. jogging after me.

"What?" I said, sighing as he caught up.

"Well, uh, I was just wondering," he began.

"Wondering what?" I said, jamming my hands into my pockets.

"Well, uh, if maybe you might want to go to the movies with me, after all," he said nervously, glancing at me.

My stomach twitched.

He really was cute. And so normal. So *not* Tobias.

He had almost certainly never eaten a mouse. On the other hand, he'd never morphed a sperm whale and gone to the bottom of the ocean while his brain was reeling with barely suppressed terror, just so he could look out for me.

I opened my mouth to say, "Sure." Instead I said, "Hey, do you speak English? How many ways do I have to say 'no'?"

He called me a name I've been called before. Then he took off. I was pretty sure he wouldn't ask me out again.

<Hey, he was cute,> Tobias called down from the sky.

"Oh, shut up, you mouse-eating freak," I said.

Tobias laughed. He knew better than to take me too seriously. <I heard that! Heard what he called you, too. The guy is perceptive as well as cute.>

"I know. I'm gonna go get some wings and come on up there. Keep an eye out for me."

<I always will,> he said.

Television. Or as most humans say, TV.
Ah, yes: TV!

I never expected it to be so compelling. At first I thought it would only be useful. I would watch the behavior of the humans on the flat, square screen and listen to them speak. When I am in human morph, I need to be able to seem entirely human.

But it is so much more than merely useful. It is a window into the human soul. Technologically it is laughable, of course, but when you take into account the stunning array of programs, it rivals the cinnamon bun itself as the finest creation of human society.

Tobias, too, enjoys TV. He comes every day to watch a show with me. It is called *The Young and the Restless.* It is very educational, though I remain confused as to the cause of so much restlessness.

TV allows me to observe much more human behavior than I see at the mall. I am still wondering why humans put their mouths together. And why they seem to enjoy it. My first thought was that they were transferring food. But that seems not to be the case.

<Look, Tobias! Victor and Nikki are doing that thing again!> I pointed at the screen. <They do this very often.>

<Uh-huh.> His hawk eyes were trained on the little screen as Victor tightened his arms around Nikki. <It's called kissing, Ax-man. Just like yesterday. And the day before. Kissing. Everyone does it. Of course, you need lips.>

<I know what it is called. And the role of lips is self-evident. I simply do not know *why* it is performed.>

<Ah, Well . . .> Tobias rearranged his wings noisily. <It's definitely got a purpose. By the way, Marco's heading this way.>

<Yes, I know,> I said. <I saw him two minutes ago, although he is trying not to be seen.>

<I heard him *three* minutes ago and saw him *four* minutes ago,> Tobias said.

Tobias is competitive when it comes to his senses. His hearing and sight are both better than mine. But I am able to look in all directions simultaneously, something he cannot do.

<You did not,> I said.

<Did so,> Tobias countered.

"Nothing likes the joys of daytime TV, huh?" Marco said, stomping up through the underbrush.

<Did not,> I said to Tobias.

Marco grinned at me. "Snuck up on you, didn't I?"

<Yeah, right, Marco,> Tobias said tolerantly.

Marco laughed. He knew he had not surprised us. His claim to have snuck up on us was human humor. It is inexplicable, and Andalite readers should simply resign themselves to never understanding.

<And by the way, why are you not in school, young man?>

"Hey, I can't be controlled by 'the man's' arbitrary schedules. I come and go as I please. I am free. No one holds me down."

<Teacher conference?> Tobias said.

"Yeah, they let us out early. So. What's on the tube? Is this . . . Whoa! Who's *that*? And does she always walk around wearing a towel?"

<Well, I'm hungry. I gotta go find a mouse. See you, Ax-man. Later, Marco,> Tobias said, and then he spread his wings and was gone.

"Watching a soap, huh?" Marco said, nodding his head.

<Soap?> I was confused. <No. This show is about humans who are both young and restless.>

Marco sighed. "Whatever you call it, it basically reeks, you know. I think it's time I introduced you to some better programming, Ax. *Buffy. Party of Five*, maybe. *Cops. South Park.* Something, anything better than this. Although *she* is hot."

<Yes, she is hot. This is why she often wears less artificial skin.>

"Yeah, well, I think you may have your cause and effect turned around there. Hey, you know what you need? A *TV Guide*."

I bristled. <I understand how to operate the TV. Human technology is —>

"Take it easy!" Marco held up his hands. "Everything with you has got to be literal. *TV Guide* is a little book that tells you what shows are on, and when. Come on, I'm bored. Let's cruise."

The notion of a guide to all that TV had to offer was attractive. But I would have to morph my human form to go into the town.

<Perhaps we could obtain cinnamon buns as well,> I suggested.

"Why not? Maybe we'll run into Jake at the mall. He can buy."

Every morph is a surprise. The last time I morphed to human, my own more or less humanoid parts, my head and arms, changed last. This time they were first.

I felt teeth growing beneath my lower face. In fact, my entire human mouth, consisting of a hinged jaw, teeth, tongue, and saliva-producing glands, was fully formed before lips appeared.

Lips form an open hole in the bottom third of a human face. The hole is used for eating and for forming mouth-sounds. As well as kissing, spitting, vomiting, and belching.

Humans do a great deal with their mouths, most of it rather pointless.

My more numerous fingers disappeared, melting into ten stronger, thicker human fingers. My stalk eyes retracted into my head, leaving me unable to see behind me without either turning my head or turning my entire body.

My front legs shriveled away, leaving me to perch precariously on my two hind legs. Of course, humans have only two legs, and no tail at all. So they go through life constantly on the verge of falling over.

My blue fur was the last to go, replaced by my own particular shade of human skin. Human skin comes in a variety of shades, none of them attractive.

At least not to me. If you are a human, you must find something attractive about your fellow humans. Humans who are young and restless are almost continuously in a state of attraction to others.

When I was fully human — awkward, slow, and devoid of natural weapons — I put on my artificial skin. Humans call it clothing.

"I am ready," I said, making mouth sounds. "R-r-r-ready. Red. E. Red. E."

"How about putting on a shirt?" Marco asked.

"The men who are young and restless do not wear shirts. I am young. And I am occasionally restless."

"Ax?"

"Yes, Marco?"

"Put on a shirt."

I did. Then I folded my scoop down so that nothing, including the TV, would be visible. Not even to a human walking directly over the spot.

I walked with Marco out of the woods, across the farthest fields of Cassie's farm, and toward the mall. It took a long time. Humans walk slowly, a result of having only two legs and no tail.

We crossed fields and then walked along a street — a path for cars. Then . . .

"Well, hello, Marco. Hey, Ax," someone called.

Marco stopped short and looked around, turning his entire human head in order to see in different directions. "Who said that?"

"Here, Marco."

I turned my human head to follow the voice. It was a truck painted with the word *FedEx*. And it was talking to us.

Warning: This Product May Alter Your DNA.

ANIMORPHS

K. A. Applegate

The Yeerks have entered the world of bioengineering: They are working on a drug that prevents human expression of free will.

The test drug has been approved for distribution...in hamburgers. The only way for the Animorphs to get inside the operation is to morph into the very cows being led to slaughter. Will they stop the experiment? Can they destroy the drug?

ANIMORPHS #28: THE EXPERIMENT

Watch Animorphs on Television!

http://www.scholastic.com/animorphs

‹Know the Secret›

ANIMORPHS

K. A. Applegate

❏ BBP0-590-62977-8	#1:	The Invasion	❏ BBP0-590-49436-8	#17:	The Underground
❏ BBP0-590-62978-6	#2:	The Visitor	❏ BBP0-590-49441-4	#18:	The Decision
❏ BBP0-590-62979-4	#3:	The Encounter	❏ BBP0-590-49451-1	#19:	The Departure
❏ BBP0-590-62980-8	#4:	The Message	❏ BBP0-590-49637-9	#20:	The Discovery
❏ BBP0-590-62981-6	#5:	The Predator	❏ BBP0-590-76254-0	#21:	The Threat
❏ BBP0-590-62982-4	#6:	The Capture	❏ BBP0-590-76255-9	#22:	The Solution
❏ BBP0-590-99726-2	#7:	The Stranger	❏ BBP0-590-76256-7	#23:	The Pretender
❏ BBP0-590-99728-9	#8:	The Alien	❏ BBP0-590-76257-5	#24:	The Suspicion
❏ BBP0-590-99729-7	#9:	The Secret	❏ BBP0-590-76258-3	#25:	The Extreme
❏ BBP0-590-99730-0	#10:	The Android	❏ BBP0-590-49424-4		‹Megamorphs #1›:
❏ BBP0-590-99732-7	#11:	The Forgotten			The Andalite's Gift $4.99
❏ BBP0-590-99734-3	#12:	The Reaction	❏ BBP0-590-95615-9		‹Megamorphs #2›:
❏ BBP0-590-49418-X	#13:	The Change			In the Time of Dinosaurs $4.99
❏ BBP0-590-49423-6	#14:	The Unknown			
❏ BBP0-590-49423-6	#15:	The Escape	**Also available:**		
❏ BBP0-590-49430-9	#16:	The Warning	❏ BBP0-590-10971-5 The Andalite Chronicles $4.99		
			❏ BBP0-439-04291-7 The Hork-Bajir Chronicles $12.95		
			❏ BBP0-590-68183-4 Animorphs 1999 Wall Calendar $12.95		

$4.99 each!

Available wherever you buy books, or use this order form.

Scholastic Inc., P.O. Box 7502, Jefferson City, MO 65102

Please send me the books I have checked above. I am enclosing $_____ (please add $2.00 to cover shipping and handling). Send check or money order—no cash or C.O.D.s please.

Name_____ Birthdate_____

Address_____

City_____ State/Zip_____

Please allow four to six weeks for delivery. Offer good in U.S.A. only. Sorry, mail orders are not available to residents of Canada. Prices subject to change.

ANI698

http://www.scholastic.com/animorphs